Dare to Dream

Iron Rogue 2

Erotic Romance

Sandy Sullivan

Erotic Romance

Dare to Dream – Iron Rogue 2
Copyright © 2018 Sandy Sullivan
E-book ISBN: 9781944122478

First E-book Publication: November 2018
First Print Publication: February 2019

Cover design by Dawne Dominique
Edited by Ariana Gaynor
Proofread by Maranda Raven
All cover art and logo copyright © 2018 by Sandy Sullivan

Dedication

To the fans of rock.

DARE TO DREAM

Iron Rogue 2

Sandy Sullivan

Copyright © 2018

Chapter One

"No! Shit! Tag, come back here!"

Dishes shattered with a large crash, shards flying in all directions. Tables tipped over, falling like dominos. Chairs skidded across the concrete, finally lying on their backs as the patrons jumped to their feet, several with food on their laps and drinks spilled across the tables, as a calico tabby cat raced past.

Alex Rockly leaned down, nabbed the ball of fluff by the scruff of his neck, and brought it to his lap, stroking the now purring cat from head to tail. He'd always had a way with animals and women.

"I'm so sorry. I can't believe he did that."

Alex glanced up when a busty brunette slid to a stop next to his table. Her hair was cut pixie short, spiking at the back while the front framed her face. Eyes the color of the sky right before a storm blew through, and lips pouty enough to give the impression she liked to be kissed, made up the whole of her face. Her body screamed made-for-orgasms as he took in the curve of her bust, the gentle scoop of her waist, and the flare of her hips—something he could totally get into holding onto. "No problem." Alex climbed to his feet, holding out the ball of multiple colored fur for her to take into her arms. "I'm glad I could help." He looked behind him to the mess the cat had left behind in his wake before focusing on the flush of color on the woman's cheeks.

Dressed in a pair of cutoffs riding low on her hips, a white tank top hugging the curve of her breast, and barefoot, she looked the epitome of casual in a sea of business suits and colorful people that made up New York City. Cars honked as they zipped by barely missing pedestrians lining the curb waiting to cross the busy streets. Sunlight reflected off the buildings as the sun began to set behind the tall brownstones on one street and the storefronts on the other. The eclectic mixture of people, sounds, smells, and atmosphere is what made the city spectacular.

"My apartment door had been left cracked open, and he took advantage, racing out to check out the city streets."

"Smart cat. New York is an interesting place."

She shifted the cat in her arms before holding out her hand for him to shake. "Madison Avery."

Shaking a woman's hand was new to him, but what the hell. "Alex."

"Nice to meet you, Alex." The cat began to squirm in her arms as if he wanted to skate away again. "I guess I should get him back upstairs before he gets loose again. Plus, I need to come down here and help them clean this mess up." She took a step back and walked several steps away. When she glanced back over her shoulder, she gave him a tentative smile and a small wave.

The door to the apartment complex two doors down from the restaurant opened with her key and she disappeared inside. *Intriguing.* He returned to his seat, sipping the cup of coffee he'd left sitting on the table in his retrieval of the disobedient feline. A raise of his hand brought the waiter closer. "Top it off please. It's grown a little cold."

"Certainly, Mr. Rockly. Can I get you a piece of cake or pie?"

"Sure. Cheesecake, please."

"Very good, sir. I will be back in a moment." The waiter started to move away, but turned back toward him. "I do apologize for Ms. Avery and her cat."

"Does that happen often?"

The man flushed red as he nodded. "At least once a week. She's a great girl, but she can't keep those cats corralled very well. One escapes frequently and we seem to be their preferred choice of escape route. She has to work off the debt of the broken dishes by waiting tables sometimes."

The waiter disappeared through the glass doors as Alex looked down the concrete sidewalk toward where Madison had disappeared. Definitely not the type he usually was attracted to, but he was charmed by her cuteness. How many of the women he'd known in the past would have raced across the sidewalks of New York City in their bare feet to catch a cat?

He'd meant for his time in the city to be productive. The break in touring with his band Iron Rogue due to personal issues their lead singer had been dealing with, made it a forced hiatus he'd planned to take advantage of. Breaks were rare in their business.

Years ago, he'd purchased a place in New York for a retreat from the farm country they'd all come from. Iowa was home, but he craved the fast-paced life of the metropolis every now and again. The people were his inspiration, giving him something raw to draw upon for his music. Noah was their lyrics master. Alex gave their songs the melody. It had been some time since he'd written anything worth a shit.

His personal life sucked. Sure, the life of a rock star had its moments. The women, the alcohol, the touring, it all seemed fantastic in the beginning. Lately, he'd become disenchanted by it, feeling the loneliness of waking up with a different woman all the time, never even remembering her name, much less anything else about her.

He squinted into the setting sun as he watched a young man rush past, his briefcase clutched in his hand. The guy looked like what a businessman should be, all pressed and spit-shined.

Alex glanced down at his own attire. Dressed in an AC/DC T-shirt, a holey pair of jeans, and a pair of black boots, he looked like a rock star. His long blond hair tied at the nape of his neck, several tattoos snaked across his arms, and the stud in his ear might give people in Iowa pause, but not here. He fit right in surrounded by the lights and sounds.

"Here you go," the waiter said, leaving his cheesecake at his elbow and refilling his coffee. "Anything else I can get you?"

"No, this is fine. Thanks."

The guy inclined his head and moved off to take care of other patrons. Alex didn't have to worry too much about people making a big deal of him while he stayed here. There were famous people all over, and he figured the locals saw them all the time.

The mess from the escapee brought a smile to his lips. Some of the people in New York needed a good shake up at times. It didn't hurt to throw them a curve ball now and then. Madison brought a smile for different reasons. She intrigued him, not something he'd had happen in quite some time.

Bringing his fork to his mouth, the smooth taste of the cheesecake slid along his tongue. Bitterness followed as he sipped his black coffee while he took in everything around him. People rushed in every direction, some heading home from work while others were dressed to the nines, making their way out for the evening. Restaurants lined the walkways along the crisscrossing streets, some with tables out on the sidewalks where patrons could enjoy the warm evening while they had a glass of wine before going to a musical. Multiple story buildings stretched into the sky several blocks away. Some of the biggest businesses in the world were based here, making New York the capital of modern trade. Two blocks up the street might be a totally different story.

Central Park wasn't far away with its tree-lined paths stretching in never-ending loops going in several directions. Some paths had flowers galore, blooming in a rainbow of colors while others led to open areas where families played.

Alex enjoyed the variety of New York, but today his interest was with a curvy brunette.

His cell phone rang in his pocket. "Hey, Noah. What's up, man?"

"How are things in the big city?"

"Great."

"Have you been writing?"

"Not much. I have some notes playing over in my head that I need to get down." Alex grabbed a napkin next to him and jotted down a few bars. "It's probably nothing, but we'll see."

"You never know. I didn't think I had a new song in me either, until I met Tori."

"She's a great girl."

"Yeah." The line crackled a bit on his end before Noah's voice came through again. "Are you going to be back to rehearse?"

"We still have a month before our first gig, right?"

"Yeah."

"I'm going to stay here and relax. I need to unwind."

Noah laughed. "Unwind in New York? That's rather funny."

"Ha ha." He inhaled sharply as he noticed Madison step out onto the sidewalk. "Listen, I need to go. I have an errand to run. Catch you later."

"Okay. Call me tomorrow, we'll touch base."

"Sure," he said absently as he climbed to his feet, threw a few dollars on the table and clicked off his phone. His steps took him behind her as he followed her down the block.

Her ass looked amazing in the pair of skinny jeans and heels she'd changed into, the cheeks filling out the denim material to perfection with the slightest jiggle to entice him. A large purse hung from her arm as she hurried down the street like she had a purpose.

A red light stopped her at the corner for a moment while she glanced both ways and then headed across the street. *New York City at its finest.*

He almost lost her on the next block when she darted into an eclectic little shop where wind chimes hung in the window, a multitude of knickknacks lined the shelves, and incense burners abounded. From his view outside, the top of her hair bounced from one side of the shop to the other.

The need to figure out what about her intrigued him so much, he stepped inside only to be bombarded by a thousand mingling scents, sights, and sounds. A low, almost Bohemian music played in the background as he tried to locate her in the shop. Following a cute giggle toward the back, he rounded the corner to find Madison wrapped in some kind of brightly colored scarf.

With his shoulder against the doorframe, he watched for several moments as she turned this way and that in front of the mirror while she chatted with a sales girl.

"Oh. I'm sorry, sir," the girl said as she moved toward him. "Is there something I can help you find?"

Madison turned, her cheeks pinking up nicely. "Well, hello."

"Hi." His gaze shifted back to the sales girl. "No. I found what I was looking for. Thank you."

The girl looked at Madison and then back to him. "Maddie?"

"It's okay, Cin. This is Alex. I met him at the café down from my apartment a little while ago when Tag got out again."

Her friend cocked her head to the side, giving him a once over that almost made him feel uncomfortable. "I see."

Madison took a few steps toward him. "Were you looking for me?"

"Actually, I was."

Her eyes widened, the blue becoming darker in its intensity. "Tag didn't get out again, did he?" She laid the scarf down on the chair next to her. "Crap. One of the others?" She grabbed her purse, walking quickly toward the door. "I'd better check. Thanks, Cin. Catch you later for coffee?"

"Sure, sweetie."

Alex quickly caught up with her a few steps from the shop. "Madison, no. I'm sure the cats are fine. I followed you into the shop hoping to talk to you."

Madison stopped and turned toward him, stepping in close enough he could see the freckles across her nose. "I'm sorry. You wanted to talk to me?"

"Yes."

Her eyes narrowed as her gaze swept over his face and hair before traveling across his chest. "Why? Guys like you don't look twice at girls like me."

That statement took him aback. Why wouldn't guys look at her? She was gorgeous with her fair complexion, pert nose, and kissable lips. Something about her had him questioning his sanity while he treaded on unfamiliar territory. "Why wouldn't I want to talk to you? You seem nice enough, unless you are some kind of stalker weirdo waiting to steal my underwear or something."

A snort escaped her mouth before she could stop it. "Just ew, okay? Underwear is not my thing."

Did she really not know who he was? Iron Rogue was the biggest thing to hit the rock scene in decades, maybe since The Rolling Stones, and she didn't know Alex Rockly by sight? That almost hurt his ego, a little.

"I thought I could buy you a cup of coffee."

She tilted her head and narrowed her eyes again, taking several moments to study him like a bug on the hot sidewalk. "Are you a model? Maybe an actor?"

He felt a grin lift his lips. "No."

She tapped her fingertips to her lips as she studied him a little longer. "I'm not into the celebrity thing. I could care less, but I don't need all the hoopla that goes along with celebrities." She leaned in, looped her hand through his arm, and placed her palm along his forearm. "Coffee it is, Alex." They started walking down the street toward the café on the corner where her cat had raced through earlier. "I really need to help them clean up."

"I think they are done by now. The other waiter said you work there?"

"Sometimes for extra cash. New York is an expensive place to live, especially down here, plus my cats get out frequently and I end up paying for broken dishes." She shrugged her shoulders and smiled. "A lot."

The sun had begun to set behind the tall buildings, bathing everything in a yellow glow. Heat radiated off the concrete still, warming them as they stopped near a table and he held out her chair. If he wasn't anything at all, he was raised a gentleman.

"Thank you. How very thoughtful."

Pleasure surged through him, making his heart race a little faster. Never one to worry about how his actions affected others, he was surprised at the intensity of his reaction when his minuscule gesture brought a smile to her lips. "You're welcome." He took the chair opposite hers, tucking the napkin onto his lap. "Would you like anything but coffee?"

"Coffee is fine."

The waiter appeared at the edge of their table. "What can I get for you?" He glanced at Madison. "Oh, hey, Maddie."

"Hey, Charles. I'll take coffee with cream please."

"Sure and for you, Mr. Rockly?"

"Coffee as well, thanks."

"Coming right up."

As the waiter moved away, Alex's gaze found Madison's again. He liked what he saw, a whole lot. The intelligence in her eyes, the way she met his gaze directly, the curve of her jaw, and the way she leaned forward as if her whole focus was on him alone, made him want to know everything about her. "What do you do here in New York, Madison?"

"I work with software."

"Like computers?"

When she smiled, her whole face lit up. "Yeah. Something like that."

The waiter brought two cups, a pot of coffee, and some creamer. The scent of freshly brewed coffee smelled wonderful even though he'd had a cup shortly before following her down the block to the shop.

"Thank you," he said as the waiter finished pouring both cups.

"Can I get you anything else? A sandwich, a salad, or maybe a bowl of soup? We have an awesome creamy chicken on special."

Not taking his eyes off Madison, he answered, "No thank you. We should be fine."

The waiter nodded before slipping away, leaving them as alone as they could get on the crowded street.

Madison stirred a dollop of cream into her coffee. "What about you, Alex? What do you do here in New York?"

He let a few moments tick by, trying to decide how much to reveal if she *really* didn't have a clue to his identity. "I'm a musician."

Her fingers came up to play with the earring in her left ear, rolling it between her fingers where it dangled next to her neck. "I see. What do you play?"

"Lead guitar."

"Do you write music as well?"

"Yeah."

The spoon clinked against the side of her cup while she continued to stir. He preferred his black.

"I've known a few musicians before and those that play guitar generally write their own music too."

"I mostly write the melodies. My friend writes the lyrics."

A smile formed on her lips, lifting the corners slightly. A dimple at the right corner of her mouth peeked out. "Interesting arrangement."

"It works for us."

"Do you live here in New York? I don't believe I have seen you before."

There it was. Casting the line, hoping for a bite. "I don't live here full time, no."

"I detected a Midwest accent to your speech."

He raised his hand, palm out to face her. "Guilty as charged. Iowa born and raised."

Her eyes twinkled with mirth. "A farm boy, huh?"

"To the core." He took a sip of his coffee before putting it back down on the table. "What about you? Born and raised New Yorker?"

"I do live here full time, but no, not a native." She tapped her fingernail against her cheek for a second. "I'm originally from Idaho, home of the potato."

He couldn't help himself. He laughed, wondering how two people from similar small-town upbringings could find each other, come together to rescue a runaway feline, and find common interests in such a large, diverse place? The idea of finding out more about Madison's hidden wants and desires held him spellbound. What would it be like to taste her skin, reveal her treasured needs, and tear a groan from her mouth when he found the one spot that drove her wild?

"Home of the potato, huh?"

"Yes. Aren't you intrigued?" A throaty laugh escaped her lips, soft and sexy as hell.

"More with each passing second."

The rim of the coffee cup met her bottom lip, and her gaze locked with his over the edge of the ceramic. Curiosity sparkled in her eyes, and his was piqued too. She could be a model with her curvy figure and gorgeous face. Her interests lie in sitting behind a monitor all day, or so he thought. He really had no idea what someone who worked in software did, only that it had to do with computers. Not that he didn't have his own technology type stuff, his cell phone, his computer, his big screen television, and social media, but the interworking's of computers baffled him.

He reached across the expanse of the table, running his fingertips over the end of her index finger. Her eyes widened and then darkened. Goosebumps rose on her arm, telling him she wasn't immune to his touch. "I'd really like to get to know you better, Madison."

In the space of a heartbeat, with the utterance of one word, she shut him down. "No."

Chapter Two

What the hell is wrong with me? This man is gorgeous, and he wants to get to know me better.

"I'm sorry, Alex, but the answer is no." She withdrew her hand from under his intoxicating touch, balling up the napkin in her lap until her fingers hurt.

"Why not?"

Her gaze focused on the dregs of coffee in her cup. *Why not? The question of the day.* When she raised her eyes and focused on his face, she took in everything about the man from his long blond hair, to his expressive eyes, and killer body. His chest was broad, his shoulders wide, and his hips trim. If he thought she hadn't noticed him before, he had another thing coming. The moment he'd snagged Tag, she'd been enthralled. When he'd stood to hand the wayward cat back to her, she'd noticed his tapered fingers, wondering what he did for a living that caused the calluses. He wasn't overly tall for a guy, but his frame was about six feet of pure unadulterated gorgeous male specimen. He could grace magazine covers with those looks.

But in the end, he didn't come across as the settling down type and she needed that, wanted it with every fiber of her being. She'd done the one-night stands. She'd done the short-term boyfriends. Her mantra now was more, more, more. The brass ring lay just out of reach, taunting her with the two point five kids, craftsman style house, and white picket fence.

Her career was set. She was one of the top software developers in New York, and she could name her price on jobs. Her penthouse apartment with her ten cats had become her sanctuary, her world inside the world of business. The waitressing she did at the café was for nothing more than a change of pace. Most of those she knew from waiting tables had no idea who she was or of her success. They only knew her as Madison or Maddie, the cat lady.

"You seem like a nice guy, but I'm kind of involved with someone." *Fucking liar.*

"Oh. I see," he said, leaning back in the chair as his gaze raked over her face. "A serious relationship then?"

Her brow furrowed as she tried to maintain the lie. "Sort of."

The fingers of his left hand caressed the handle of his coffee mug, reminding her of how he'd touched her moments before and how her body had reacted to that touch. His eyes narrowed as he took her in. He didn't believe her. She could tell by the crooked grin now lifting the corners of his mouth. Did anyone ever tell the man no? Probably not, she decided. It was time someone did. "I'm a very busy person. I don't have time to date."

"Who said anything about a date?"

Confusion rushed through her brain. He didn't want to take her out? "What exactly are you wanting then?"

"A mutual arrangement. Spend some time together. Have a little fun." He leaned forward, dropping his tone to almost a whisper. "I'm only in town for a short time. It's lonely in the city without company. I'm sure I could make your time worthwhile."

Did he really just proposition me? The man definitely has an ego the size of Manhattan Island. "I'm sure there are plenty of women who would jump at the chance to spend some time in your bed. I, however, don't have the inclination to become a notch on your bedpost, belt, or cock. I don't play games, Alex, and I'm done with one-night stands. I'm pushing thirty, I'm set in my career, and quick flings are something I gave up five years ago." She climbed to her feet. "Thank you for the coffee. I hope your stay here in New York is a pleasant one."

Moving around the table, she pushed out a breath and kept walking all the way back to her apartment complex door, swiped her keycard, and popped open the glass panel. The audacity of the man was more than she could even fathom. Never in her life had someone assumed she could be bought and that's exactly what she'd felt Alex hinted at.

"Damn. I was really hoping he'd be different, but it is what it is, I guess."

The elevator door slipped open with a *whoosh*, showing her an empty car as she stepped inside and pressed the button for the top. As the car slid to the top, the numbers on the illuminated box above the door moved by at a clipped pace, she leaned back against the bar behind her, stuffing her hand inside the pocket in the front of her shorts. She should have known with his looks and killer body, he'd be all about immediate gratification. Disappointing, to say the least.

Tag rubbed against her ankles, and she bent down to pick him up. His soft fur tickled her chin as he brushed up against her face. "Such a troublemaker, you are mister." The rumbling of his purring body vibrated against her chest, bringing a smile to her lips. She did love her furbabies, all ten of them. It was a good thing she had a big apartment.

Taking the cat with her to the kitchen, she set him on the floor and started mixing up something for supper. She hadn't really eaten today except a muffin for breakfast. Saturday's were her day to relax and read. Today had been different with her run-in with Alex, but tonight would be marathon movie night, she'd decided. Patrick Swayze was on tap and Dirty Dancing was one of her favorite movies. Ghost was on after that.

The steak in the sink defrosting since morning would make a great meal on the grill she kept on the balcony. With her apartment being on the top floor, she had her own small rooftop garden outside the sliding glass door in her living room. The place had cost her a fortune to buy, but the bonus she'd received with her move to the city a few years ago, made it all possible. Who knew little Madison Avery from Pocatello, Idaho would become a multi-millionaire by writing a program that would save big business billions in production costs by stream-lining their inventory programs.

She'd always loved computers, everything about them actually, but her passion had become figuring how to make them do what she wanted. She'd also been in on a new game that had gone viral the moment it hit the stores last year. The gamers of the world had gobbled it up, making it the hottest thing to hit the gaming community since Call of Duty. She was set for life if she invested wisely, which she had every intention of doing. Her investment broker brother made sure of that.

The sliding glass door opened with slight pressure from her hand as she took the plate she carried outside to fire up the grill. The garden boasted a wicker couch, several wicker chairs, a small gas fire pit, and lots of plants, some flowering, some not. It was her Zen place, somewhere she could disappear when stress had her in its grasp and wouldn't let her go.

The grill heated quickly while she admired the setting sun over the city. The lights below slowly flickered on as the sky darkened, turning orange, red, and purple. Once she had the meat on, she went back inside to work on a salad and a baked potato to compliment the meal. She did enjoy her red meat. Steak medium rare had always been her favorite.

The salty, spicy searing meat smell made her mouth water as she waited for it to be done to perfection. She went back inside to get the potato out of the microwave and fix her plate so the moment the steak was done, she'd be ready to eat. Her stomach growled at the thought.

A slight breeze kicked up, picking up the ends of her hair as she stepped back outside. The cooler air had goosebumps rising on her arms, making her wish she'd brought a sweater outside with her, but no matter. She would enjoy her food in peace before she kicked back in front of the television.

Lifting the lid to the grill, she checked her food and then glanced across the street to the apartment building directly in line with hers.

Her stomach dipped when she noticed the man standing on the balcony. She couldn't see his face, but the long blond hair gave away his identity now that she knew.

Alex.

The heat of his gaze fixed on her as he stared, not indicating he'd seen her, and not moving a muscle. She could feel the intensity of his eyes from her head to her toes. Her skin prickled with awareness, the same way it had done when he'd touched her hand downstairs at the café. A shiver raced down her back, and she was acutely in tune with the way her body hummed like a live wire.

He leaned forward, his forearms braced on the railing, his hair cascading over one shoulder. The light coming from his apartment shadowed his face, although she could feel every touch of his gaze as if he'd actually stroked her skin.

The sizzle of meat juice hitting the flame brought her attention back to her food, making it easier to breathe.

When she glanced back across the street, he was gone.

Breathe. Breathe.

With the steak on her plate, she disappeared back into the apartment, leaving it sitting on the table as she grabbed a glass of wine. Tonight was going to be a full bottle night.

The sweetness of the red slid across her tongue, the perfect complement to her food. Drinking wasn't a huge deal most of the time, but the rush of energy she felt right now had her needing something to chill her out or she would never sleep. This intense attraction to a man was new to her, very new. Most of the time sex was something she could do without. Her vibrator seemed to satisfy her needs. Right now, she had a strange feeling, tonight, it wouldn't be enough.

Once she finished eating, she rinsed off her plate and stuck it in the dishwasher. The every other day load would be ready to run soon. Living alone didn't require much for housework, dusting every now and then, vacuuming every few days, and making her bed every morning seemed to be the extent of it. Without a husband or even a significant other, she didn't need to be real tidy.

Turning off the lights, she walked to the balcony door and peered out. Darkness surrounded everything other than the lights of the city. Alex's apartment was pitch black, no illumination to be found at all. *He's probably out picking up some other girl from one of the local bars.* The thought actually hurt.

With her glass in hand and the bottle of wine in the other, she walked through the sliding glass door and took a seat on the wicker couch, tucking her bare feet up under her bottom.

One thing she missed about living in the country was the stars. New York didn't make it easy to see them with all the bright colored marquees lighting up everything from the street to the tops of the buildings.

After a few moments, the barest sound met her ears. The soft melody of a guitar played a song she didn't know.

Time seemed to stop as she listened, unsure if it was coming from where she thought it might be. Surely it wasn't Alex.

Squinting into the darkness, she focused on his apartment trying to make out any movement. Nothing stirred inside or out. White gauzy curtains swayed in the breeze, giving off a ghostly appearance.

A figure stepped from between the glass doors and the curtains, bare-chested and clutching a guitar as he sat down in a chair. *Alex.*

Leaning forward to catch sight of him, Madison held her breath, waiting for the sound to reach her. The haunting melody speared her heart, making her want to hear his deep voice sing the entire song. The whisper of the notes slipped along her skin.

The wine glass made a slight clunking sound as she put it on the table beside her and brought one of the thick pillows to her chest. Her breaths came out in a ragged pant, her lungs burning with each breath. Lord, she was so turned on, she could hardly think much less move back inside and forget all about the intoxicating man across the street. What would it be like to have all of that focused on her? His callused fingers brushed over her electrified skin would feel intense. His eyes burning through her as he brought their bodies together in one powerful thrust of his hips, would shatter her into little pieces. His hair, all that glorious hair curtaining them as he bent over her running his tongue along her spine.

Oh, God.

She needed to go inside, but she couldn't move, couldn't think. If he knew she watched, she could never face him again. If he had an idea she now slipped her hand beneath her pants, sliding her finger over her clit as she shuddered with pleasure, he would probably tip his chin up and grin, knowing he'd brought her to this state. Her body wasn't her own anymore, it was his.

A moan escaped her mouth, forcing her to clamp it shut to stifle the one right behind it. Her eyes fluttered shut, her thoughts centered on the notes of the guitar. Her clit became slick with her desire, and her finger slid easily over the hardened nub. Thoughts scattered, all except one. Alex.

His voice came to her on the breeze, unsure if he really had spoken or if it was her imagination. Either way, her body reacted in a way she wasn't familiar with as his voice whispered, "Come for me, Maddie. Fly apart for me and let me feel your desire on my mouth."

The shattering cry she couldn't hold back split the night air. The guitar stopped, her breath held waiting for something, anything. When it began again a few seconds later, she sighed, hoping he had no idea it was been her screaming out her orgasm to the night sky above New York City.

If he knew she'd been thinking of him when her orgasm rolled over her, she'd have to avoid facing him at all cost. His type had an ego a mile wide without her stroking it until he glowed with it.

* * * *

Alex smiled to himself as he began to strum the guitar again. He knew Madison sat on her balcony across the street. Her cry of pleasure was something to behold when it had flown from her lips a few moments ago. There weren't too many women he'd been so turned on by that he'd had to pleasure himself in the shower, but she was one. Right now, his dick hurt almost as much as before he'd taken things in hand. He might have to make another trip under the running water.

Not aware of her position in the apartment building, he'd been surprised to realize she owned the penthouse when she'd stepped outside to grill her food and glanced at him standing on his. She hadn't acknowledged his presence although he knew she watched and when he'd come outside with his guitar and began to play, she'd listened after she'd turned out the lights.

A secret lingered between them, the secret of the mutual attraction he'd felt downstairs. Denying it would be futile. Pursuing her would be a pleasure he hadn't experienced in a while. The lifestyle he'd become accustomed to leant itself to women throwing themselves at him and the guys. The pursuit would be sweet. The treasure in the end would be sweeter.

Darkness shrouded him from her view. He knew she could hear the guitar melodies, even across the busy street below, but he wondered if it was the music or him that made her come apart with a cry. Had she even been aware his name had sailed from her lips as she'd climaxed?

The whoosh of her sliding glass door closing stilled his fingers. The song he'd been playing didn't have any lyrics nor did it have a title, but he knew it was good. The notes were something he'd been working on for some time, unaware of how they fit together. Tonight, the entire song materialized in its entirety without a lot of thought on his part.

His inspiration had gone to bed apparently, although he could see a light flickering in a window a short distance from the balcony jutting out toward him. *Her bedroom.*

Another light, deeper inside the window came on, her shadow passing in front, blocking it out for a second as she moved inside and closed the door to what he assumed was her bathroom.

What he wouldn't give to be the one soaping up her gorgeous body, running his hands over her slick flesh to give her more pleasure than she'd ever experienced before. His hands would slip over her breasts, stopping to thumb her nipples to hard peaks. Water cascaded over his shoulders as he placed open-mouthed kisses on her shoulder, moving slowly down to take one of those nubs into his mouth.

One hand would disappear between her sexy thighs, to find her wet and needy. Her cry of pleasure at his touch had him aching and ready to come.

A soft moan left his lips as he pressed his hand to his rock hard cock. Good Lord, he ached to be inside her. He needed relief and soon, but he didn't want just anyone. Taking himself in hand seemed pitiful, even to him. It had been a very long time since Alex Rockly hadn't had a woman at his beck and call. His list of willing waiting women took up a lot of pages in his little black book. There were several he could call who lived here in New York. That thought had an empty feeling to it.

His fingers flew over the guitar strings, plucking out the tune he now couldn't forget. Good thing he could retain a song from memory only.

A smile crept over his lips as a plan formed in his mind. He'd have to pull some strings, but he wanted that woman more than anyone he'd ever had the pleasure to meet. By damn, he would have her until he got his fill and then move on, the way he did with every other woman he'd ever met. His heart was not in the mix, never would be. First, he'd have to find out more about her, likes, dislikes, and things that turned her on. She'd be eating out of his hand inside of a week and splayed out on his bed shortly thereafter.

If dating was the way to get her there, so be it.

The pad of paper he'd brought outside with him sat on the table. Pen to paper, he began making a list of things he'd need.

Flowers.

Limo.

A romantic dinner on the roof. Candlelight. China. Catered food since he couldn't cook a lick.

Black suit. Funny because he hadn't worn one of those since high school. His normal attire consisted of tight t-shirts, jeans or black pants, and big boots. Occasionally you'd find him shorts or sweats when he worked out or went for a run in Central Park.

Theater tickets.

A pretty piece of jewelry.

She'd be pure putty.

His cell phone rang and when he picked it up, he saw Aiden's name. "Hey, dude. What's up?"

"I thought I'd check in with you. I haven't heard from you in a couple days." Aiden cleared his throat. "What's up in the Big Apple?"

"Not much. I got a new song down."

"That's fucking awesome, man. We need some new stuff. Noah's kicking out some great lyrics. You two need to get together and bang it out."

"It can't be sappy though. Noah's stuff is all about finding love and that shit."

Aiden chuckled. "He can't help it. With Tori in his life, that's the way he's feeling."

"I know, but man, our fans want raw, savage shit, you know?"

"Yeah, although they do like the love songs sometimes too. Do you want to play me what you have?"

"Sure."

Alex banged out the melody of the new song until he realized parts were slow and methodical even though other pieces were hard and rattling.

"Uh, dude?"

"Yeah?"

"You do realize you have some soft, sappy shit in there too, right?"

Alex sat in silence for a second before saying, "Yeah. What's up with that? I'm not in love with anyone."

"Met anyone new in New York maybe?"

"No. Well, actually yeah. I have a neighbor across the street I met today. Seems nice. Killer body."

"But?"

"She turned me down."

The roar of laughter coming through the phone had him frowning. Aiden apparently found that as funny as hell. Him, not so much. It sucked, actually.

"Not funny, man."

"It is, Alex. You haven't been turned down by a woman since Iron Rogue hit five years ago."

"Fuck you."

"It's true. Women throw themselves at your feet. They are usually so wet by the time you get around to fucking them, you can't keep your dick inside."

"She's different."

"Obviously."

Alex glanced across the street. No lights shone in Madison's apartment. A sigh escaped his lip as he pushed his fingers through his hair. "I can't use the *I'm the lead guitarist for Iron Rogue.*"

"Why not?"

"She doesn't know who we are or who I am."

"You're shitting me."

"Nope. Apparently, she's not into rock."

"What the hell does she listen to, then?"

"No idea, although I get the impression she might be more of a classical type girl."

The notes of Beethoven drifted across the street. *Definitely classical.* No wonder she had no idea who he was.

He couldn't deny the fact that he was at a loss as to how to go about this whole thing. Women loved being wined and dined, right? "I have a plan."

"A plan?"

"Yeah. I'm going to take her to the theater, have someone cater a nice candlelit dinner on the rooftop, by her flowers, you know, all the romantic shit."

"That might work."

"Maybe."

"Hell, I don't know, man. You're asking the wrong guy. I don't have a clue either. Maybe talk to Noah and see what he did to get Tori into his bed."

"It was Noah, dude. Tori used to orgasm to his voice. What the fuck do you think he did?"

"You sing too, just not often."

"I don't have a voice like Noah's though."

"Maybe not, but yours can do it too with the right song."

He remembered Madison coming apart earlier with a cry of his name on her lips as he played his guitar. Raw rock might be what tripped her trigger and she didn't know it. Life was about to get fun because he planned to find out her weakness and use it to his advantage.

The seduction of Madison Avery had begun.

Chapter Three

The doorbell rang at Madison's apartment the next morning. No one ever visited her, and she hadn't ordered anything to be delivered to her house.

"Coming," she said, leaving her computer desk in the office down the hall.

When she opened the door, she was surprised to see a huge bouquet of flowers held by someone only visible from their waist to their toes.

"Uh. Can I help you?"

"Madison Avery?"

"Yes?"

"I have a delivery for you."

The flowers were gorgeous. Several purple roses, daisies, and other flowers she couldn't identify were arranged in a fantastic crystal vase with lots of fern and baby's breath mixed in them. "Are you sure you have the right place? I don't know anyone who would send me flowers."

"Yes. Madison Avery. Penthouse apartment. Hillridge building on Seventy-Eighth Street," the man said peeking around the flowers.

"Well, okay. Bring them in and set them on the table there." She stepped back, allowing the man inside where he put the vase on her coffee table. The arrangement damn near took up the whole table.

"Where do you want the rest?"

"Rest?"

"Yes. I have six more vases in the hall on a cart."

"Holy shit. Six?"

"Yes, ma'am. Apparently, someone wanted to make an impression on you."

"I guess so."

Once he had them all in the house, he pointed out that each card was numbered one through six. "You are to open each card in sequence."

"This is really odd but okay." She grabbed card number one, tapping it against her lips for a moment, trying to get up the nerve to find out who sent them and find out their purpose. "Thank you," she said, handing the man a tip for his trouble.

Tucking her feet under her, she sat down on the couch staring at the handwriting on the front of the card. Her name scrawled across the envelope looked very bold and self-assured.

Her fingers shook as she slipped one under the flap, popped it loose from its glue, and pulled out the card.

Six p.m.

"What the hell?"
She grabbed card number two.

Candlelight

She grabbed card number three.

Dinner

Number four proved a little hard to find. It took a minute since it had been buried in the flowers.

You and me. Alone

The fifth card almost pissed her off although it was kind of sexy how demanding the notes were.

Wear something sexy, off the shoulder, clinging, and short. I want to   see you.

The last card revealed who had decided to play this game with her. Her hand shook as she glanced down.

I can't wait to see you. Alex

What did he think he could do, order her to be at his beck and call? *I'll be damned if he can tell me where, when, and how. The next thing he'll be doing is telling me to spread my legs so he can do whatever he pleases whenever he pleases.*

"How arrogant!"

She stood up and began to pace.

"Damn him. I'm not one of his groupies who will fall at his feet and kiss his boots." Yes, she knew who he was, all six foot of the gorgeous lead guitarist for Iron Rogue. She'd known he owned the place across the street from the moment she'd moved in it. Had it been a deciding factor in her buying the place, no. It didn't hurt though. Disappointment had been a constant companion for a few weeks when she realized he rarely used the penthouse apartment.

When she'd almost tripped into his lap downstairs the moment Tag had gotten loose, she thought she'd die. Then, he asked her for coffee. She'd said yes, hoping beyond hope he wasn't the egotistical rock star everyone made him out to be. He was every bit.

She wanted different. Obviously, it wasn't meant to be.

Maybe it was. The flowers didn't seem to be a typical rock star thing. Of course, if he'd never been told no, this was new to him and he was falling back on the old standby of flowers, dinner, and some romance, hoping he would get lucky. She wasn't stupid by any means, and this was a typical man move.

Now, she had to decide if she would play into his scenario, eat his food, drink his wine, fuck him until tomorrow, or take those first couple of things and go back to her apartment alone. The second scenario wasn't as fun as the first, but she didn't want to be another woman he fucked and walked away from.

Being a little hard to get wouldn't hurt him.

He hadn't given her his number, but she obviously knew where he lived. Cautious of being hurt, she'd play this easy. The last thing she needed in her life was a brooding rock star.

Excitement had her body humming to a new tune, something she didn't recognize. What would it hurt to use him just as he planned to use her? Nothing, she decided. After all, he probably could use some humility in his life.

She glanced at the clock. It was barely ten and she had a full day of work in front of her. That had to be her focus for now, but she could hardly wait to see his face when he opened the door tonight. The perfect killer dress hung in her closet, one she hadn't worn for quite some time. Tonight, it would be his kryptonite. He wanted sexy, he was going to get sexy.

Her computer pinged with a message, telling her she needed to get back to work if she planned to cut off early to get ready.

When she shot a look at the chat window as she sat down, she rolled her eyes even though no one could see her. Her asshole boss needed something *again.* As the senior programmer for the company, she pretty much set her hours and her jobs based on what she had going on, which for her didn't mean a whole lot. She rarely went out except once a week to lunch with her brother who made sure she knew what an inconvenience she was to his banker schedule. He asked her every week if she was seeing anyone. No would be her reply.

He'd have a coronary if he found out about Alex, even if she couldn't say they were dating.

Were they dating?

Did this constitute as a date?

He said he didn't date, so what did that mean?

She covered her mouth with her hand to stifle the giggle that threatened to erupt. Alex would set her brother off and send him to the depths of hell with his long hair, tattoos, and everything that she thought went with the rocker lifestyle, the women, the booze, and the drugs.

Google popped up on her laptop with a few taps of the keys.

Alex Rockly.

Images flooded her screen.

She should be working, but instead, she was stalking her neighbor. What a creeper she'd turned into.

The man didn't lack for female companionship if the pictures said anything at all. Arm wrapped around a blonde, leaning in for a kiss on a brunette, arms cradling a redhead. Good grief, the guy was a manwhore. She couldn't blame him, really. He could have any woman he wanted, so why in the hell was he asking her out to wine and dine her?

He surely wasn't desperate for a fuck.

No way.

She opened the band's website. Lyrics to their songs were under one tab. Another held candid photos of the guys, making her laugh at some of the faces Alex made when the camera wasn't a professional one. A third tab held the store where fans could buy their CD's, t-shirts, and several other items of paraphernalia. She held her breath as she opened the tab labeled tour schedule.

This would tell her approximately when he was leaving New York again.

As she scrolled down to the bottom, the date popped up. Three weeks from today was their next gig.

On the west coast.

Shit.

Her email pinged again. Her boss. Damn it.

She opened the chat window, blowing out a long sigh as she attempted to focus on work for the rest of the day when her mind wasn't on computer programming in the least.

Three hours later, her cell jingled by her elbow. The name Maxie flashed on her screen.

"Hey, babe. What's up?"

"You."

"Me? I haven't done shit in days." She tapped out a few more commands on her computer, before scrolling down and bringing up the entire program to tweak what she'd put in.

"Have you seen the website for Rock Band News today?"

With the phone cradled between her shoulder and her ear, she said, "No. Why would I?"

"You are all over it."

"What the hell are you talking about? Why would I be on Rock Band News?"

"Is there something you aren't telling me, chickie?" Maxie was her best friend in the world. They'd moved to New York together where Maxie became a top model in the fashion industry, working exclusively with one of the most popular fashion designers in the city. At six foot and all legs, her friend stopped traffic on 5th Avenue whenever she made her way around the city. Madison felt dowdy next to her gorgeous friend, but Maxie wasn't the least bit pretentious and she loved her friend like a sister.

"I tell you everything, woman."

"Then why are you staring starry-eyed at Alex Rockly, the drop-dead lady killer from Iron Rogue?"

"Holy shit. You're kidding me, right?"

"I wouldn't kid with anything like that. When did you hook up with him?"

"I haven't. Well, not really. Tag got out of my apartment the other day, and Alex is the one who rescued him at the café."

"And?"

"Nothing."

"I can tell when you're lying, girl, and you aren't giving me the whole truth." Maxie left the silence for a moment on the line. "Spill it."

"He asked me out for coffee. That's it."

"Bullshit."

Madison blew out a breath. "Okay, fine. He sent me flowers today, and we're supposed to have dinner tonight."

Maxie squealed on the other end of the phone. "Oh my God, Madison! He is so hot, he could melt the asphalt on the street."

"I know, right?"

"This is so cool. You're dating Alex Rockly."

"Whoa. Back up. We are not dating."

"He's taking you out for dinner and you're not dating? What did I miss?"

Madison explained everything that happened with Alex since she'd met him officially downstairs. "You see, so we aren't dating."

"Sounds like a date to me."

"Alex Rockly doesn't date, Maxie. He fucks women and then drops them at the curb of their place as he puts another notch on his belt."

"Are you going to let him do you? I totally would, you know."

"Maxie!"

"I would."

"I'm not sure if I can. I mean, yes he's built like a brick shit house, but I want more. You know that."

Maxie's voice dropped to the pacifying tone she loved to use with Madison. "I hate to say it, babe. I don't get the impression Alex would be the white picket fence type."

"I know," Madison whispered. She didn't want to read anything into the dinner with Alex, but her heart wanted to hope there was more to it than him just trying to get her into bed. She glanced at the clock. "Shit. I need to go, Maxie. I'm supposed to be ready by six and it's already five. I have to shower, change, and do something with my hair."

"Need me to come over?"

"Would you? I could use your expertise with my makeup and hair. You know, I suck at them and you're an expert."

"I have people that do mine."

"Yeah, but you were always better than me."

"I'll be over in a second but only if I get to meet Alex."

Madison didn't know if she wanted her friend anywhere near Alex. What if he thought Maxie was who he wanted and not her? What if he dropped Madison like a hot rock when he talked to her friend?

"Maddie, you know I would never take your man away, right?"

"I'm not worried about you. I'm worried about him. I know his reputation."

"Maybe he's not really like they make him out to be, or maybe he needs to find the right woman to settle down. That girl could totally be you."

"Right, but I love you for saying that." She closed down her computer before rising to her feet. "Okay. Get your butt over here."

"Five minutes. Find the dress you want to wear and put it on. He won't know what hit him."

God, she loved her friend.

True to her word, Maxie showed up on her doorstep five minutes later as Madison hopped on one foot while she tried to slip on her heels. When she opened the door, Maxie whistled softly.

"Okay?"

"Babe, you'll have him eating out of your hands."

"Really?" She smoothed the clinging material over her hips, wishing they were a bit smaller, her stomach was flatter, her boobs were bigger, and that she hadn't cut her hair the last time. Guys liked long hair, right? "It's not too slutty?"

Maxie's eyes got really wide before she headed down the hall. "We are talking about Alex Rockly. Nothing is too slutty for him." She plunked down the makeup bag she'd brought on the bathroom counter. "You've seen the women he's been with."

"Pictures, yes, but I don't want to be one of them."

"That is totally on you, Maddie. If you don't want to be, then don't. Make him work for you." Maxie pulled her in front of the mirror and turned her around. "Tip your head up here so I can work."

"You're six foot. I'm five-five. There is a bit of a height difference there."

"Work with me, girlfriend, work with me."

Twenty minutes later, Maxie turned her around.

"Holy shit."

"I know, right? You look gorgeous."

"That's me?"

"Yes, babe, it is totally you and Alex will be tongue-tied." Maxie touched the corner of her mouth to wipe a small smudge of lipstick off. "Go get him."

The buzzer on the intercom grated along her nerves as she glanced at the clock. Six on the nose. "Yes?"

"Madison?"

"That's me."

"It's Alex. Can I come up?"

Now, he asks? "Uh, sure. Top floor."

"I know. See you in a minute."

Her stomach flip-flopped with a mind of its own as goose bumps broke out over her whole body. What the hell was she thinking? This was Alex Rockly. He didn't date plain girls from

Idaho. He dated models, gorgeous women who would look good on his arm and make him more popular than God.

The doorbell rang a moment later as she blew out an unsteady breath and glanced at Maxie who held up two thumbs with a smile plastered on her face. Mouthing a *you got this* to her, Maddie couldn't help but smile in return.

After a second ring of the bell, Maddie put her hand on the knob, took it off to blow on her sweaty palm for a moment, and then returned it to turn the knob.

The man standing on the other side of the door had his back to her, but the moment she turned around her breath stopped, it wasn't Alex.

Chapter Four

At least not the Alex she expected. His hair was tied back at his neck, cascading to his waist in a long ponytail. His eyes were clear and bright, staring back at her with appreciation as they raked down her frame in a sensuous sweep that had her panties wet. The man had on a suit. Alex Rockly wore a suit—for her.

The smile lifting the corners of his mouth revealed straight white teeth with a slight tilt of his lips to the right. "Wow," he whispered, stepping inside to shut the door. He planted a kiss to her cheek. "You take my breath away."

"Thank you."

A second later, his gaze fixed over her shoulder, stopping on what she knew had to be Maxie and her stomach dropped to her toes. It was as she thought. He would now fawn all over her friend and forget Madison was even in the room.

When she turned, she was shocked to realize he hadn't moved and his attention was totally focused on her.

"Who is your friend?"

Embarrassment flooded her cheeks. Maybe she'd overreacted. "This is Maxie Reynolds. She and I are best friends from back home. We moved out here together."

Alex held out his hand, taking Maxie's in a handshake. "Nice to meet you, Maxie. You look familiar."

Here we go. "Maxie is a fashion model."

"Ah, that's probably where I've seen you then." He slipped his arm around Maddie's waist, totally taking her by surprise. "Any friend of Maddie's is a friend of mine."

"Alex. It's nice to meet you as well. I am a fan of your music."

"Fantastic. I hope you'll like the new songs we will be releasing with the new album."

"You have new music coming?" Maxie asked.

"Yes, with the new tour."

"Will you be somewhere close, I hope?"

"Our first show is—"

"On the west coast," Maddie replied at the same time, but before she could cover her lapse in judgment, Alex shot her a look, one she couldn't really read.

"You know our tour schedule?" His gaze fixed on her face as one eyebrow rose over his left eye.

Stupid, really, really stupid. He thought she didn't know who he was, or she'd given him that impression, and now she'd totally blown it by opening her big mouth. "Not really. I looked today and saw where the first show was."

He grinned as he pulled her a little closer, leaning in to whisper, "You're busted, babe. You knew who I was the minute we met." He rubbed his nose against her ear. "We can talk about that later." When he focused back on Maxie, Maddie couldn't do anything but stare. "Let me know if you're going to be in the area, and I'll get you tickets."

Maxie bounced on her toes in excitement. "That would be awesome."

"We should go. Don't want to be late for dinner." Maddie followed him to the door where he grabbed a sweater she had hanging on a hook and slipped it over her shoulders. "It might get cool on the roof."

"We're eating on the roof?"

"Yes, my roof."

Her voice was nonexistent as she let him lead her out, his hand at the small of her back. Maxie closed the door behind her with a click, walking out with them until they hit the elevator and the doors slid open.

"You two go on. I'll catch the next one."

The door slid shut, enclosing them in the all-glass box, their reflections casting an odd image back to her. Alex was quite a bit taller than she was, but as he brought her into the cradle of his arm, she leaned closer taking everything about this night to be a one-time thing. Expectations after this were nil in her book. He wasn't the type to go beyond one date.

"Maxie seems nice."

"She is."

"How long have you been friends?"

"Since second grade. I was the nerdy girl in the corner. She came over and sat with me at lunch. We've been best friends ever since, and when I got my job offer in New York, she came with me. It didn't take her long to surpass me with the success. She's a top model in the city now."

The elevator slid open, revealing the lobby of her apartment complex. Brass fixtures adorned the walls, with large planters holding plants and flowers covering almost every corner. Two small marble steps down took them to the exit where he pushed the door open to the cooler night air.

Cars sped by, honking as pedestrians tried to cross the streets between them. The whole city always seemed in such a rush. People walked swiftly by, heels clicking on the concrete sidewalk while they kept their eyes straight ahead, not even glancing to the side.

Alex guided her to the corner with a hand to her lower back, where they waited for the light to change. "Do you like living in New York?"

"Not always. I like a little slower pace sometimes, but it is exciting to see the sights and people of the city. I do like the park though. It's nice to go walking through there in the mornings."

The light changed before they stepped off the curb headed for his side of the street. His building looked very similar to hers. The old world charm of the San Remo area of New York drew her in every time she came home. The large building with its twin towers reaching for the sky made her feel nostalgic in a way. Celebrities owned most of the apartments, people who had more money than they knew what to do with. Rumor had it that Demi Moore owned one of the penthouses. Her building was on a smaller scale, as was Alex's, but impressive nonetheless. Living across from Central Park had been a dream of hers from childhood.

Like hers, Alex's building had a doorman who swept open the large wood encased door as they approached.

"Evening, Mr. Rockly."

"John. Nice to see you."

She leaned in close. "Wasn't he here when you came to get me?"

"No. They changed shifts about fifteen minutes ago. John does the night shift."

"Oh. I'll never get used to having a doorman."

Alex pushed the button on the elevator. "Neither will I. Growing up in Iowa surrounded by cornfields, we didn't have doormen."

She laughed, thinking about having a smartly dressed man opening the door to the home where he'd lived as a child. "Did you have a big house?"

The whoosh of the door opening on the top floor startled her for a moment until she realized they'd arrived. The ride up sped by with barely a notice of the movement of the fancy car.

"Not really. We didn't do the farm thing, preferring to live near town. My dad worked at a factory nearby and mom was a housewife, taking care of us kids until we all moved out on our own." He opened the door to the apartment near the end of a very long hallway, the lights coming on automatically as they stepped inside.

The space was gorgeous. A long marble staircase swept up, curving to the right as it made its way to the top. Beneath their feet, the black and white tile in a checkerboard pattern glinted in the light reflecting from the massive chandelier over their heads. Off to the left was a library where books lined the huge cases along the back walls and large windows reflected the night lights of the city. To the right was a dining room. The eight-person table in the center already set for a dinner party looked unused and out of place.

"Do you really live here?"

A smile lifted the corners of his mouth, revealing a teasing grin. "Sometimes." He guided her forward through an arched doorway into a sunken living room where dark furniture and walnut tables dominated the space. Every area they came across lacked personal touches.

Her own apartment seemed small but comfortably messy with her clothing scattered about, photos of family and friends on the walls, and brightly colored pillows giving the space texture and brightness.

Aromas assaulted her senses. Rich dark scents that tantalized her nose with something she couldn't quite place.

"Close your eyes," Alex said, stopping her at the door to his balcony.

"Okay." She did as he asked, taking a moment to bring all the intoxicating smells into her to place the one uniquely his.

A blindfold slipped over her eyes, effectively blocking out everything and keeping her from peeking.

Spicy yet with a hint of musky male. *Alex.* Behind her eyelids she could picture him clearly. His eyes, his hair, his straight nose, and full lips tipped in a sexy smile.

With her hand in his, she heard the slide of the door right before the night air hit her face with a crisp chilling breeze. Goosebumps rose on her skin, from anticipation or the cold, she wasn't sure.

"I'll warm you up."

Her heart sped up double time, waiting for him to guide her where he wanted her to go.

"I won't let anything hurt you." He led her out the door as she fought the urge to put a stop to his tantalizing game. This was his space, his sanctuary, where he'd played his guitar the night before, bringing her to orgasm with nothing more than his melodies.

The seat of a chair met the back of her thighs. "Take a seat."

She heard the scrape of another chair being pulled across the concrete floor of the balcony.

"I debated on how to approach our date tonight."

"Is it a date?"

"Yes. Why do you ask?" His mid-western drawl intrigued her, making her wish she could know him outside of the hustle and bustle of the city.

"My understanding is Alex Rockly doesn't date."

A soft chuckle drifted on the night breeze. "That brings us to the fact that you knew who I was all along. Why the charade?"

"I'm sorry I deceived you. I am not one to be dazzled by famous people. Yes, I admit I knew who you were the moment we met, but it didn't change my opinion of you one way or another, nor did it sway me in any way to accept your challenge of tonight."

His fingers slid along her forearm where it rested on the arm of the chair. A shiver rolled down her back, her body on high alert to his touch.

"Why did you accept?"

"I don't remember accepting or denying."

He leaned closer, his lips a mere whisper from her ear, ruffling the wispy hair lying at the side of her neck. "You let me into your building. You are wearing something similar to what I asked you to wear. You were ready at the specific time, allowing me to bring you here, to my apartment. I would think that was acceptance in the truest form."

Her breathing became ragged, a desperate sawing of air while she tried to still her rapidly beating heart. "What do you want from me, Alex?"

"Want? That is a very strong word, Madison."

"Want, need, desire—all the same thing."

"Not in my book."

A chill settled over her as his heat moved away. "Can I take this cloth off now?"

"No," he replied from a distance she couldn't fathom. "Dinner is ready."

"I can't eat blindfolded."

"I'm going to feed you."

Her breath stopped. Feed her? Like a pet, a puppy or kitten maybe?

The clank of a plate being set on the table reached her ears. Other noises, unfamiliar, but intriguing made her hyper aware of everything around her. The sounds of passing cars on the street below were slightly muted. The buzz of neon lights flickering off and on could be heard over the din. The clopping of horses' hooves from the open carriages along Central Park was a welcome sound, the sound of home.

Tines of a fork touched her lips. "Open."

Letting her tongue wet her bottom lip, she opened her mouth as Alex slipped the fork inside. Taste buds burst with flavors of thyme, oregano, bay leaf, garlic, and—spaghetti sauce.

She chewed for a moment, relishing the flavors of Italian cuisine on her tongue. "I love Italian."

"I'm glad," he said. "It is one of my favorites too."

A hard crust of bread touched her lips as she opened to take in a small bite of the garlicky melted butter. Alex brought a glass to her lips, allowing her to take a sip of a sweet wine.

The whole feeding her thing seemed intimate, almost too intimate. She barely knew him, remembering the tidbits from entertainment magazines she gleaned over the past few months.

He dated blondes. He liked women with big boobs, hers weren't huge by any means even though she thought they were a nice handful. He wrote music, mostly melodies for the band. He grew up in Iowa where he'd known the other guys of Iron Rogue since high school. She didn't think he'd ever been serious or in a long-term relationship before. He owned this apartment and had for about a year. He only came to New York infrequently.

"What's going through that brain of yours? I can almost see the wheels turning."

"I'm trying to figure you out."

"Fat chance. No one has yet."

"Can I take this off?" She touched the blindfold. "Although this is sexy and fun, I would like to be able to see you when I talk."

The blindfold fell away, revealing just how close he sat to her and hiking up her awareness of the man tenfold. He'd pulled a chair up beside her, one of his knees on either side of hers. The warmth of his body penetrated her skin, heating her from the inside out. He'd removed his suit jacket, revealing a crisp white shirt hugging his broad shoulders. His forearms were bare where he'd rolled up the sleeves, his tattoos bright against his tanned skin. His hands were braced on his thighs, the fingers long, slender, and callused from gripping the strings of his guitar. The ends of his hair flicked slightly in the breeze that surrounded them, making it look like they were dancing to their own tune.

"Hi."

"Hi."

"So talk."

Silence held her, unable to unroll her startled tongue to form any words beyond the mundane greeting.

She swallowed, more for something to do than to wet her throat, giving her a second or two more to gather her thoughts as she stared into his eyes, those expressive eyes. The corners of his mouth lifted in a little grin, drawing her gaze to the fullness of his bottom lip. Scruff lined his jaw, a little darker in color than his blond hair.

Would it tickle against my skin if he were to kiss me?

"I love your eyes on me, Madison, but you have questions?"

She cleared her throat as she brought her gaze back to his. "You don't do relationships. Why me?"

He leaned back in his chair. "This is a date, not a relationship. But to answer your question, no, I don't do relationships. I don't really date much either. I am more of the guy who gets seen by dating the women who get me seen. It's part of the music business game. We are always in the limelight. It gets tiring at times."

"Tiring?"

"Yeah. Sometimes it is nice to be normal. We don't do normal much. It's why we go home on occasion, back to Iowa where everyone already knows who we are, so we aren't the anomaly. We are the guys who went to high school there."

"I see. That would get old."

His eyes twinkled in the candlelight she hadn't been aware of until now. The whole scene looked light something out of a romantic movie. A string of bare bulbs hung above their heads, dancing in the breeze like fireflies on an open field of pasture grass. His balcony was good sized, with dark wicker furniture, a long table with a glass top, and several potted plants.

"To answer your question of why you?" A shrug lifted one shoulder. "You intrigue me. You didn't treat me any different than any other guy you'd met on the street. I'm not used to that. Women usually are ready to jump into bed with me the moment they meet me. They don't brush me off."

"I didn't brush you off."

"You did. I hardly got the time of day from you." He brought another bite of spaghetti to her mouth before taking a bite from her plate for himself. "You are a beautiful woman, someone who takes life a little too seriously, I think."

The spaghetti went down a little hard, making her take a sip of the wine to wash away the lump. He took the glass from her hand and brought the exact spot she'd placed her lips, to his own. The heat in his gaze when he looked over the rim at her, had her panties melting into a puddle between her thighs. The man was sex on a stick.

God help her because he appeared to *want her.*

His fingers trailed up her bare calf until he lingered on her inner thigh.

"I want to get to know you, Maddie. *Intimately.*"

Her body felt like it was about to combust into a puddle of goo right there on the chair.

Intimate with Alex Rockly? Yeah, she could do that and more, but where would that leave her in the morning.

* * * *

Alex could almost feel the heat coming off Madison, to the touch of his hands on her. She quivered under the brush of his fingers, making his cock hard as a damned rock. He couldn't wait to be inside her sweet heat, her cunt snug and warm around him. "What kind of things do you do for fun, Madison?"

It took her a moment to focus on his question rather than his hand on her thigh, her eyes cloudy with desire already.

"Uh, walk in Central Park, go to a museum, have lunch with a friend, nothing too exciting."

Her breath came out in a silent sigh as his hand climbed higher. He could smell her arousal, the sweetness on the air a heady scent.

The trails of his fingertips up her arms brought goose bumps in their wake, chasing his touch up to her bare shoulder. "You have a gorgeous neck." He climbed to his feet, bringing her up with him only to tug her into his arms as he swayed to the music he'd programmed before their night began. Her head came to just under his chin. "You dance beautifully." His hand rested at the small of her back, sliding gently over the bare skin revealed by the cut of her dress. Soft, silky, and so tempting, he could hardly control the need to bare more of her.

"It's not hard when the man you are dancing with has rhythm."

A chuckle left his mouth. "I have never been accused of not having rhythm."

They moved like they'd been dancing together for years, her body cradled in his embrace perfectly.

Her skin glowed in the moonlight, tempting him to taste what beaconed him. The brush of his lips on her shoulder made her shiver beneath his mouth. Open-mouthed kisses forced a sigh from her lips as he continued up the side of her neck to her ear. Her skin tasted better than he could have imagined, something sweet and delectable he couldn't seem to get enough of. Little nips of his teeth brought her breathing to a stuttering stop for a moment.

When he moved back, he looked down into her eyes. Glazed over with passion, her gaze fixed on his. Her lips were parted slightly, tempting him beyond the craziness of the instant, he couldn't deny what he wanted, to taste the sweetness of her mouth.

His hands came up to cup her face, cradling her jawline in both hands. Her fingers gripped his forearms as if she tried to hold him in place. Pushing him away wouldn't have been an option, he needed this, needed her right this second more than his next breath.

The air ignited between them, sparking like lightning to dry grass, setting everything around them ablaze with color. His skin felt alive where she touched him, something he'd never felt before.

She waited, still and expectant.

Their breaths mingled into something almost tangible, heady and on fire with need.

His lips finally touched hers with a soft mere brushing of skin against skin. Her mouth was exquisite, tasting a little of the wine she'd drunk and a lot like Madison. He tilted her head to get better access, sliding his lips over hers, taking, savoring, and then devouring her as he took the kiss deeper. A soft whimper escaped her lips as her fingernails dug into his forearms.

One hand slid to the base of her neck, cradling her head in his palm, his fingers tangling in the hair there, holding her for his onslaught. Lips, teeth, tongues, everything crashed together in a desperate need to get closer.

His hand wandered down her back, cupping her ass to hold her tighter against his body. His cock ached, a slow burn settling at the base of his spine.

Pulling back, he nipped at her lips every few seconds, not wanting to stop kissing her, but knowing they needed to take this into the other room. He didn't want the first time with Madison to be a quick fuck on the wicker furniture of his deck.

Her eyes slowly opened, alight with a desire for him that took his breath away.

He had her right where he wanted her. "My bedroom is through those doors. Let me bring you pleasure beyond your wildest dreams."

A frown made the little wrinkle between her eyebrows more pronounced as the haze of need cleared from her gaze.

Conflict reflected back at him, something he wasn't used to. Women didn't tell Alex Rockly no.

Chapter Five

It took a moment for the cloud of physical attraction Alex had woven around her with his sensual kisses to clear. Going to bed with him tonight would be a mistake she would regret for a long time to come if she wanted more than just a quick fling with a hot rock star.

What did she want? A relationship with him seemed a farfetched idea, but one she couldn't shake. She'd bought her apartment knowing he owned one nearby. The day they'd met officially, she had made sure he was aware of her as a woman, not only a chick off the street or some groupie who followed him everywhere. Those were a dime a dozen in his world. He'd said so himself.

Her dilemma now was should she give in, take the one glorious night of being in his arms, or should she deny herself, and him as well, the pleasure and hope for something more? If she turned him down, would he come back for more? Did she take the chance?

She smoothed her hand down his chest, feeling the ripped muscles beneath his shirt.

"Maddie?"

The sound of her name on his lips sent a shiver of desire through her. What would it sound like in the throes of passion? How would it feel to hear it as he came apart?

When she raised her gaze back to his, she saw the confusion in his eyes. He wasn't used to being turned down.

"This can't happen."

"Why the hell not? You're attracted to me. I can see it in your eyes, and I want you more than my next breath." He ran his finger down her cheek. "I can feel the way you shiver under my touch." A smile lifted the corners of his mouth, revealing a slight indentation in his cheek she wanted to run her tongue over.

"Believe me, I am so hot for you, I can barely think, much less function." His fingers played with the curve of her ear. "We can enjoy our moments together, the few they are, and cherish the memory as we move on with our lives."

Okay. Fuck that. I want more than a few stolen moments. She stepped back out of his arms. "Sorry. I love myself more than to be a few seconds in the life of Alex Rockly, lead guitarist for Iron Rogue."

On shaky legs, she turned toward the door and headed for the front of his apartment to let herself out.

As the door clicked closed behind her, she leaned against the wall while she waited for the elevator to take her down.

Dare to dream. Her mantra for life. Well, she'd dared to dream of something more than one night with Alex and it had blown up in her face. Tomorrow would be a new day, one she would make the most of and forget about what might have been with the rock star across the street.

Morning sun warmed a path across her cheek as she opened her eyes to stare smack into the slanted gaze of Tag. "Well hello to you, Mr. Escapee," she said, scratching the multi-colored feline behind the ears. "I suppose you want to be fed?"

A deep purring rumbled along the cat's body.

"I'll take that as a yes."

She flung back the covers and threw her legs over the side before climbing to her feet only to be surrounded by the other nine residents of her apartment, all meowing for their morning grub.

"All right, all right. I hear you." Her cell phone lay on the bedside table, the time lighting up the screen with a bright seven a.m. "I guess I'd better check in soon."

Cell phone in hand, her steps took her down the hall and into the massive kitchen with the huge window over the sink where she could see Central Park. A slow drizzle of rain sent a long line of water down the pane to rest at the base.

"Great. Rain to go along with my bitchy mood."

The coffeepot gurgled to a stop as it finished brewing. She would need the fortification today after a restless night of sexy dreams containing her gorgeous rock star neighbor. Damn the man anyway. Why did he have to be so delectable?

After quickly feeding the cats, she poured herself a cup of coffee, taking it into the living room and setting it on the table. With her feet curled up beneath her, she stared out the sliding glass doors watching the rain come down in rivulets. She had plenty of work to do today, but she didn't have any motivation to get up and log into her computer.

Life seemed simpler before she met Alex. She didn't dream of someone touching her, kissing her senseless, or bringing her to the heights of passion before he slid inside her and made her world spin out of control. Sure, she dreamt of finding someone to spend the rest of her life with. The face of the man was always cloudy and unfocused. Now, he came into sharp clarity with long blond hair, piercing eyes, and fingers that could strum her to a screaming orgasm with hardly a touch. How she knew this, she wasn't sure.

Her cell phone warbled on the countertop where she'd set it when she poured her coffee, indicating her mother was calling. A sigh escaped her lips as she climbed to her feet and went to retrieve it. She really loved her mother, but today was not the day she wanted to hear about the guy she'd met at the gym, the new neighbor who had a son who would be just right for her, or a cute guy she'd saw on an online dating website. "Hello, Mom," she said after she'd settled back onto the couch.

"Sweetheart, it's good to hear your voice this morning. How are you?"

"I'm fine. Getting ready to start my day. How are you?"

"Oh, you know, same old, same old." Her mother said something to her dad and then came back on the line. "Listen, there is this young man I met the other day..."

Maddie set the phone down on her knee and let her mother go on with an occasional uh-huh and a no, Mother, I am not interested as her gaze fixed out the sliding glass doors.

A movement caught her attention, making her sit up a little taller while she tried to see where it was coming from.

Alex parted the curtains on his window, focusing his gaze across the way directly at hers before raising his coffee cup in a silent salute. Could he tell she was watching from her apartment? Surely he couldn't see her inside. His chest bare, he was the epitome of sexy rock god. One she hope to be snuggled up to when they awoke for the day soon. If she didn't give in to the desire for the man, maybe they could have a future together. Probably not, but a girl could dream.

She pulled at the edges of the boy shorts she wore to bed. "Listen, Mom, I have to go. I have a lot of work to do today, and I need to get started."

"Oh. Well okay, sweetie. Call me later and I'll set up a date for you with Charles."

"No, Mom, really. I don't need a date."

"Sure you do. You mope around that apartment all day without even going out for lunch or anything. You need a date."

"I have a date or had one last night. I'm good."

"You did?"

"Yes, with a really gorgeous guy I met at the café downstairs. We might even be going out again soon."

"That is fabulous, Madison. What is his name? Do I know him?"

"No, I'm sure you don't, and his name is Alex." The little white lie wouldn't hurt her mother, and it would get her off the subject for a little while. In a few weeks, she would break it to her mother that she wasn't seeing Alex anymore and that would be the end of it for a while. Her mother would have a cow if she ever met Alex anyway. He was definitely not the type she expected her daughter to go out with, much less settle down and have a family. Rock star was not on her list of acceptable job titles. "I need to go. I'll talk to you later."

"All right. Love you, sweetie."

"Love you too, Mom. Bye." She clicked off the phone and looked back out the window. Alex was gone, leaving her disappointed in herself for even wondering about him.

Work beckoned, so she might as well get to it. It wouldn't get done if she didn't. Life went on without Alex Rockly as bleak as that sounded.

* * * *

Alex sipped from his cup before putting it on the table at his knee. He needed to concentrate, something he'd been unable to do for several weeks now. Music usually came easy for him, had since he'd been young, but lately inspiration wasn't there. Unable to put his finger on the reason, he'd come to New York to spend time away from the guys in the band. Breathing room sounded good, even if it was in the middle of the hustle and bustle of the big city. People here were an interesting breed.

His cell phone rang where it sat on the table beside him. The screen flashed Dylan's name before he answered it. "Hey, man. What's up?"

"I am here in the city. Thought you might want to catch up, get something to eat, carouse around for women. You know, the usual."

"Sure. Where are you now?"

"At the airport. Got here a few minutes ago."

"Take a cab to my place and then come on up. I'm sitting here trying to get some music down on paper, but I seemed to be stalled."

"Sounds good. See you in a few."

Dylan was the drummer for the band, and one of Alex's best friends. All the guys were really. They'd meshed since high school, but since Iron Rogue became very popular in the last few years, they didn't get to spend much downtime hanging out the way they used to. It would be great to kick back. Aiden played bass and the man could play. He didn't write and he didn't sing, but his fingers could pull out the low notes of a song like no one else. Noah was the lead singer, but since he'd hooked up with Tori, they didn't spend as much time together. Alex couldn't blame him. Tori fit his friend like a glove. They were made for each other from what Alex could tell. Maybe someday he would find that kind of woman. Not that he was looking. For now, he was content making women happy in bed.

Guitar in hand, he plucked out a few more chords, shaking his head in disgust when they didn't string along with the others he had down. The whole thing sucked. He wadded up the paper into a tight ball, flinging it across the room at the overflowing trashcan sitting in the corner. He'd been at this a while without much luck. The melodies weren't coming, not like they usually did, and he wasn't sure why. It had been quite some time since he'd had this much of a block.

A sheet of paper. Nothing on it. No pencil marks, no smudges, no notes, no words. *Fuck.*

Alex laid the guitar on the couch beside him and climbed to his feet. Something had to give. This was driving him insane.

Movement to his left caught his attention. Madison's balcony. The curtains shifted and she stepped out, the sunlight glistening on her wet hair, shorts barely covering her ass cheeks, and a ripped t-shirt baring her midriff and one shoulder where it slid to her upper arm. Her nipples poked the front of the shirt. *No bra?* Ah, hell. He was screwed. His cock came to instant attention, hard and insistent against the front of his pants. The throbbing ache behind his fly reminded him he hadn't had sex in a long time. It had been over six months, actually, and that was a first for him. He never went that long without a woman. Maybe it was time to find a warm body. A night out on the town with Dylan might be the ticket.

Thirty minutes later, a knock sounded on his door.

"Come on in. It's open," he said, knowing his band-mate was probably on the other side.

Dylan sauntered through the portal and shut it behind him. "Hey, dude." His friend put his duffle bag on the chair to Alex's left before heading to the kitchen. "I need a beer."

"Man, it's only ten in the morning."

"I know, but I've been up all night, so it's like midnight at home."

Alex shook his head as Dylan pulled a bottle out of the refrigerator and tipped it to his lips. "You need to slow down on the alcohol."

"Shut the fuck up." Dylan threw himself down in the other chair next to his duffle. "You need some color in this room. It's too drab."

"What are you, the design police?"

A laugh escaped his mouth. "No. I can tell you don't live here full time. It's sterile. No wonder you can't write." He took another long pull on his beer.

"I'm writing."

Dylan nodded to the pile of crumpled paper in the corner. "Yeah, I can tell."

"Are we doing a conference call this afternoon to decide on the keyboardist?"

A shrug lifted one shoulder as Dylan's gaze moved toward the sliding glass door. "I guess. Noah mentioned something about it."

"What's your vote?"

"I don't give a shit. Any of them will do."

Alex didn't believe him. He'd seen the interest Dylan had shown in the female that had auditioned for them. A woman on tour with them might pose a few problems, but she'd been the best, by far, out of those who had come out. "Taylor seemed to be the best. She knew all of our songs and jumped right in."

Dylan jumped to his feet, moving restlessly around the room, taking several long drinks of his beer until it was gone. "I said, I don't care."

"What the hell? Why are you so jittery?"

"Sorry. I haven't slept much the last few days."

"Go take a nap, then." Alex nodded down the hall to his left where the extra bedrooms were. "We can go out later and find a couple of ladies and get laid. That should chill you right out."

The look in Dylan's eyes concerned him when their gazes met. They lacked passion like he'd lost his zest for life and was struggling to find it. Something was bothering his friend. Dylan's issue wasn't just a lack of sleep. Deeper. Alex couldn't place it, but his eyes almost looked dead.

"I guess. I could use some sleep."

"Go then. I'll sit here and pluck out some chords. You sleep."

"Thanks, man."

"You bet. I got your back."

Dylan's gait shuffled along as he moved down the hall, and Alex heard the door close a few moments later. He probably needed to call Noah or Aiden and see if they knew what was up with their friend. This wasn't like him at all.

Alex let it go for over an hour, hoping Dylan was fast asleep before he called Noah. He didn't want him to hear the conversation in case this situation called for more than a shoulder.

The phone rang twice as Alex went out onto the balcony.

"Yo."

"Hey, man."

"What's up? You don't usually call me this much."

"Dylan is here."

"In New York? What the fuck?"

"I know. Shocked put it mildly when he called me from the airport."

"That's weird."

"Yeah. Any idea what's going on with him? He seems, I don't know, off." Alex ran his fingers through his hair, from scalp to neck, finger combing the strands into submission so he could put it back in a ponytail at the base of his neck.

"No clue. He was fine when he was here, but then again, I haven't seen him much in the last two weeks. You know, with me and Tori."

"I bet."

"You should be happy for me, man."

"I am, Noah, really. I'm glad you've found a nice girl. I like Tori. She's perfect for you."

"Then why the shit?"

Alex glanced across the way to Madison's windows. Nothing stirred. When she'd been outside a little while ago, she'd stayed for about thirty minutes before moving back inside without a glance in his direction. It bothered him that she didn't seem to care that she walked away last night. "I'm not trying to give you shit. I don't know. Maybe I'm a little jealous."

The laughter that echoed through the phone line made Alex frown. Did everyone think it was hilarious that he might want to settle down someday?

"You? Jealous? There's a new one."

"I want a lady someday, you know, just not right now."

"Okay, Alex. Whatever you say."

"Fuck you. I'm calling about Dylan, not me. We are *not* discussing my love life or lack thereof."

"You haven't gotten laid lately, have you?"

It wasn't a true question. Noah knew him well and sexual frustration burned his gut raw. Six months was a long damned time without sex. "No. It's been a while."

"How long?"

Silence.

He didn't want to admit how long it had really been. Alex Rockly going without sex for a week was unheard of. Six months?

"Alex?"

"What difference does it make?"

"A lot. You don't do well without sex for a period of time."

"Six months."

"What did you say?"

A grumble under his breath revealed his frustration at the whole thing. "Six fucking months, Noah. No sex for six months."

"Why the hell not?"

"I don't know. I wish I did. I haven't been able to write anything worth shit in weeks. My sex life is in the toilet. Geez, I could use a hooker." He threw up his hand, letting it fall to his side. "I'm horny as hell. I need to hire a songwriter. And oh, if you have one handy, send me a bombshell girlfriend so the rock world doesn't think my dick has fallen off. The moment I do get some chick in bed, I'll probably shoot like a bottle rocket with a short fuse on the fourth of July."

"You might want to write some of that down. It would make for a killer song."

"You know what, Noah. You're a dick."

Noah laughed before he said some soft words to, Alex assumed, Tori before he came back to the phone. "If you and Dylan are jamming, maybe Aiden and I should fly up. We could use a little rehearsal time before the first show in a few weeks."

"If you want to. You know I have room. We could probably book some studio time at one of the dive places here in the city."

"Great. I'll make the arrangements and we will be there in a few hours. The plane is sitting idle anyway."

"Bring Tori. I'm sure she would love to go shopping here."

"I might do that, although you know how much she loves flying."

"Yeah, the puking stench still lingers in the bathroom of the plane."

"It does not."

"If you say so, bro." Alex stepped back inside his apartment and headed to the kitchen for more coffee. He needed the fortification if he was going to make it through the day. Now with the others coming too, the place was going to get crazy.

All he could think about was if the noise would disturb Maddie and her cats.

Chapter Six

Madison made it downstairs, skidding to a halt at the end of the table in the café in time to see Alex come out the door of his apartment complex followed by three other guys and a woman. Trying to be nonchalant, she took a seat at the corner table, grabbing the menu from the top, and opening it to look over the edge so she could watch what they were doing. When they got closer, she could see the guys with Alex were the other members of Iron Rogue. Not that she stalked them even though she knew more about each one than any normal woman should. The woman with them had to be the girl Noah was in love with. She was pretty with her long hair in curls around her shoulders. Their story was all the news in the rock band world recently. Maddie thought it was cool the way they'd fallen in love.

Someday maybe that would be her.

Her focus rested on Alex. Lean, tall, and oh so sexy, he stood out from the others, at least to her.

Why in the hell didn't I give in and let him make love to me last night?

Because it would have been a huge mistake. One and done. Madison Avery wasn't the type of woman Alex Rockly would look twice at on a normal basis. He usually went around with models on his arm, he'd even said so himself. She would have been a one-night diversion and that was something she wouldn't stoop to if she had her way.

"Maddie?" Alex's voice came at her from the right.

Damn it. She'd been daydreaming to the point he'd brought the group across the street and caught her.

"Uh. Hi, Alex." She glanced behind him to the group.

"We were going to get a bite to eat. Mind if we join you?" he asked, taking the chair next to her and nodding everyone else to take the chairs around them.

"Sure. I guess." Her face fused with heat. "Hi."

"Sorry. I should introduce you." He went around the table, naming off everyone and introducing her to each. "She lives in the penthouse apartment kitty-corner from mine. We met the other day when one of her cats escaped, taking out half the café in his wake."

"You have cats?" Tori asked, opening the menu but watching Maddie over the top. "I love animals, but with the touring about to start, we can't have anything over about the size of a rat."

"No yapping shits, Tori," Noah replied, pushing the hair from her shoulder and kissing the bare skin exposed. Tori turned toward him and brushed his lips with hers.

"I promise." She blushed and glanced back at Madison. "I like big anyway."

"Big it is, babe."

"Knock off the kissy face crap, you two." Dylan snapped open the menu, not even glancing at Madison.

"Jealous much, Dylan?" Aiden turned toward her, picking up her hand where it lay on the table. "I'm Aiden. Bassist for the band. It's nice to meet you, Madison." He brought her fingers to his lips, kissing the knuckles as she blushed deep. "Don't mind him. He's been in a pissy mood lately."

"Fuck you, Aiden."

"Not in this lifetime, buddy."

Alex laid his arm across the back of her chair. "Ignore them. They can be a bit rough around the edges."

"Rock stars usually are, I hear."

"She's got every one of you pegged," Tori added. "How many cats do you have?"

"Ten."

"Holy cow!"

"They do keep me busy cleaning litter boxes."

"I bet."

The waiter arrived to take their drink orders and offer an appetizer which the guys all agreed on as Maddie watched their exchange. It was apparent they'd known each other a very long time while they bantered words, talked music, and gave into the general bullshit of the day.

"Hey, Alex. Why don't you invite your lady friend to our jam session? She might find it interesting," Noah said, his fingers sliding along Tori's shoulders in an intimate caress.

Maddie almost sighed. She wanted that. Alex's fingers did a slow crawl across her shoulder, taking her by surprise. It wasn't something she expected from him at all. Alex Rockly didn't personify intimate. "How about it, Maddie? Want to come and watch us play?"

"If you don't mind. I think it would be fun."

Tori leaned in conspiratorially. "You'll love it. I watched them play when I first started seeing Noah. It was fantastic to see them unplugged."

The waiter brought their food and they all dug in like they'd been starving for weeks. Typical males. Tori had a big salad, which Maddie thought kind of funny because the girl certainly didn't need to lose weight or anything. Noah looked like he had no problem with her curves in the least. The sly glances, small touches, and whispers between them made Maddie jealous.

Her stomach rolled. She really didn't need a man in her life. Happiness came from within and she was ecstatic with everything she had. Money wasn't an issue. Friends—well she had a few, but no one extremely close to her. Family wasn't far away. Pets, now those she had. They gave her unconditional love, head-butts when she needed them, rubs against her when she felt lonely, wet noses in her face in the early mornings, especially when it was time to eat, and yeah more than enough love to go around.

Maddie picked at her burger. It tasted great as always, but for some reason, it sat like a lump of lead in her stomach.

"Not hungry?" Alex asked, his lips close to her ear.

Shivers raced down her arms. Her reaction to the man wasn't a problem. He could turn her upside down without doing much of anything. The issue was whether she wanted to let it go on into a great sex fest and let him break her in two, or deny them both and suffer from now until God only knew when. He wouldn't suffer for long, she knew, not with a woman at every turn. "Hmm. Not really. I ate not too long ago."

He grabbed a fry from her plate, popping it into his mouth. "I love fries."

She pushed her plate toward him. "Eat them before they get cold."

Shoving a few more in his mouth, he grinned as he wiped ketchup from the corner of hers and then sucked on his finger, giving her a wink before turning back to his friends.

Her body felt like someone had stuck her in a light socket and turned it on. Blood sizzled in her veins. Her legs went weak with the need for him to touch her more intimately. Her focus got lost somewhere in the feel of his finger on her face and as it disappeared in his mouth.

If she didn't kick her self-control in the butt, she would be drowning in Alex Rockly before the night was over.

* * * *

"Sit right here," Alex said, putting her on a stool near the side of their makeshift stage.

The building wasn't much more than an empty warehouse not far from where he lived, but it had been decked out inside with soundproofing. A few of the bands he knew jammed here and they were lucky to get some time this afternoon to pick a little. They even kept a few instruments for the guys to use. It wasn't their own equipment, but since they weren't doing anything to be recorded, it would work out fine.

Noah pulled him into a huddle a few feet away. "Anything new, Alex?"

"Not really. I've been writing a bit, but things aren't flowing well. You?"

A sheet of paper appeared in his hands. "I've got a few lyrics. Maybe you can do something with those."

Dylan tapped out a rhythm on the drums he'd borrowed, lost in his own thoughts.

"What's going on with him?"

"I don't know for sure." Noah glanced at Dylan. "We need to vote on who to hire for the keyboardist."

"I asked him about that earlier and he shut me down. Said he didn't give a shit."

"I think he cares more than he's letting on."

"Me too."

Noah raised his voice, giving Dylan and Aiden a wave to come over to where they stood. Once the other two were close, Noah brought up the subject. "Okay. We have six candidates for the keyboardist position. Do you three want to write down who you would like or just say a name?"

"I vote we say a name," Aiden replied. "I know who I want."

"Dylan?"

"You all vote. I don't care."

"You are part of this band, man."

"And if we all vote for someone different, we are screwed since there are four of us."

"I vote Taylor." It was clear Aiden knew who he wanted.

"I vote Taylor, too," Noah added.

Alex glanced from one man to the other. Dylan didn't look any of them in the face, just kept his gaze focused on the wall across the warehouse. The choice was clear. Taylor was the best person for the job even if it would make touring a bit different having a woman in their midst. If Tori was with them more times than not, it would make it a little easier. "I vote Taylor."

"Fuck." Dylan stomped off back to his drums and sat down. The beat he pounded out gave away his frustration at their decision.

"I'll call her and let her know. She lives here in New York, so maybe she can come by and work with us today." Noah pulled out his phone and walked away a few feet.

Aiden moved closer. "What the hell is that all about?" He nodded to Dylan.

"I'm not sure, but I think there is something up with him concerning Taylor. He couldn't take his eyes off her when she auditioned. As far as I know, they don't already know each other, but the heat simmering between them was pretty thick."

"It'll work out."

"Yeah, I guess so."

Noah walked back over to them and nodded. "She'll be here in an hour. We need to get our attorney to draw up the contract and bring it over if he can. She needs to get up to speed so she can go out with us on our first show."

"Sounds good," Alex said. "Let's get warmed up."

The minute Taylor walked in the door an hour later, Dylan's hands stopped in mid-air. Alex grinned. Their band-mate had the hots for the new keyboardist and things were about to get real if the girl would be on tour with them.

"I need a break," Dylan said, climbing to his feet and disappearing out the doorway.

Taylor's gaze followed him out. "Everything okay?"

"Yeah." Noah held out his hand. "Welcome to Iron Rogue."

Taylor's smile was huge as she shook each of their hands. "You guys have no idea. This is a dream come true for me. I can't wait to feel the excitement of the crowd when we do our first show."

They talked for a few minutes before Dylan came back in, and Taylor took her spot behind the keyboard.

"I know it's not your own, none of the stuff here is ours, but it's a place to practice a bit and see what we need to work on. Alex is staying here in New York for a few more weeks. If we need to, we can have our instruments shipped in. I think these will work for now."

Taylor played a few chords on the board, nodding in return. "This will work for me." She pulled out the melody for Dare to Love. "What do you want to work on first?"

Noah stepped to the front of the group. "Taylor, we know you're familiar with most of our songs. I don't think that's going to be an issue. We do need to go through each one to make sure we are on track. I have a playlist already made out for the first show with a few additions." He smoothed out the paper from his back pocket, handing a copy to each of them. "You all good with this?"

They all nodded.

"All right. Alex, get us started and the rest of you pick up your parts."

For the next two hours, they went through every song they had and a few by some other artists they liked. A few times they had to start over on a song to get the beat, although overall they meshed well, just like they always had.

Alex kept glancing at Maddie. Her eyes were wide with wonder and excitement. The grin never left her gorgeous lips the entire time they played. Her gaze rarely left him, something he was used to in a sense, but not from her, not from the woman he couldn't seem to get out of his head.

Sweat dripped from his temple, making a track down his face to his neck. A shower would feel really good when they got back to his place. He wondered if he might be able to convince Maddie to join him in there. Yeah, probably not. She seemed hell-bent on not giving into the chemistry between them, even though it was off the charts intense.

Sometime during the set, Tori had pulled her chair next to Maddie, and the two of them had their heads together in deep conversation as the band wrapped things up.

When the last notes drifted into the air, the two girls looked their way and his gaze caught Maddie's. Her eyes sparkled as a soft smile lifted the corners of her mouth. Her hands were clasped between her knees, like she was afraid to reach for him even though she leaned forward.

Without realizing it, he laid his guitar down and walked toward her.

"Wow," she whispered, as he cupped the back of her head and drew her to her feet. One hand on her jawline and the other still holding her head, he took what he wanted.

No preamble. No buildup. No thought.

His lips crashed into hers, taking the kiss he'd been dying to have since he caught her staring from behind her menu at the café. Her hands came up to rest on his forearms, digging into the skin with her nails. Her tongue met his in a tangle of need, their lips molding together as he took the kiss deeper. Nothing penetrated the fog of wanting her beneath him. Everything in that moment centered on her lips against his.

A shrill whistle finally broke through the haze of desire.

"Alex, man. The cab is waiting."

"My place?"

"Your friends?"

"They'll wait."

"Wait?"

He shook his head. "I need you. Right now."

"Now?"

Noah whistled again. "Alex?"

"Ten minutes. Send the cab back."

"Ten minutes?" Maddie stepped back. "Ten minutes?"

"What?"

"Oh fucking hell no, Alex Rockly. I get a hell of a lot more than ten minutes or you can find some other chick to bang the headboard with." She shoved him to the side as she headed for the door. "I'll find my own way home."

* * * *

Madison fumed, slamming the door as she entered her apartment. Pissed off was a mild term for the rage rushing through her. "The fucking nerve of the man!" She threw her keys across the kitchen island. "Ten minutes. I don't think so."

Tag rubbed against her leg before she picked him up and then flopped down in the armchair.

"What's wrong with me, Tag? I mean, all I want is a nice guy who cares about me the way Dad cares about Mom. Someone who will love me for who I am, not caring that I like ice cream on Friday night and to sit and watch a movie with him, snuggling until I fall asleep on his shoulder. I don't need some guy who is all about himself and what he wants." She stroked her hand down the cat's back, scratching him under the chin for a second. "I don't know why I thought Alex might be different. He's a rock star after all. They only know one thing and that's how to do the short-term relationship thing. Wham Bam Thank You Ma'am."

A soft knock sounded on her door. She debated whether to ignore it or not.

It came again.

She sighed, put the cat down on the floor beside the chair, and climbed to her feet. Company wasn't something she really wanted at the moment. Ben and Jerry's ice cream and a good romance novel would have been better.

"Who is it?"

"It's Tori. Can we talk a minute?"

Madison opened the door, finding Noah's girlfriend on the other side with a bottle of wine and an ice cream bag.

"I brought provisions."

"Come on in. Wine and ice cream will get you entrance anytime."

"I won't reveal that to Alex for now. He might bring a truck with half ice cream and half wine."

Madison giggled as she shut the door behind Tori. "I have a corkscrew in the kitchen. Let me grab it and a couple of glasses."

"No bowls?"

"Hell no. Spoons and the carton do for me."

"My kind of girl!"

When she returned to the living room, Tori had made herself at home, kicking off her sandals and tucking her feet under her. Madison handed her one of the glasses, letting Tori pour the wine as she opened the ice cream. They sipped and scooped for several moments before Tori put down her glass and let the spoon go idle in the carton.

Madison held up her hand. "Don't talk to me about Alex."

"I wasn't going to. Not really. I wanted you to know something. We just met, but I feel you and I are kindred spirts. If you hadn't noticed, I'm not a skinny girl, I'm not drop-dead gorgeous, and I have a big mouth. It comes with being a reporter."

"You're a reporter?"

"Used to be. Rock Band News actually. I still work for Lyric on the side doing interviews and stuff with bands."

Madison felt her face flush hot. She should have known. "Holy shit. You're a celebrity too."

Tori put her hand on top of Madison's. "No, I'm not. I'm a girl like you, who is in love with a rock star."

"I'm not in love with Alex."

Tori's eyebrow rose. "We'll leave that one alone for now, but you are attracted to him to the nth degree. It's written all over your face when you're in the same room."

Madison sipped her wine, afraid to reveal too much lest it get back to Alex.

"Whatever is said in this room, doesn't leave this room, Madison. I swear. I saw what happened at the warehouse, but I swore we wouldn't talk about Alex unless you wanted to. I wanted you to know I'm here if you want to talk. I don't know how long Noah and I will be in New York and yes, we are staying at Alex's. I promise I won't say anything more."

In love with Alex? No, absolutely not. I refuse.

"How did you meet Noah?"

Tori grinned. "It took six months for me to snag a gig doing an interview with Iron Rogue. The minute we met, he hated me. I mean literally hated me."

"No way."

The glass rose to Tori's lips, and she took a sip. "Yep. I wanted the scoop on the lyrics to Dare to Love. He refused to tell me, so I stowed away on their plane." She grimaced. "I get airsick though and started puking in their bathroom. He found me. His idea was for me to stay with them for two weeks and get the inside digs on the guys from a normal perspective. I stayed with him at his place, got the interviews, and wrote the article.

"It blew up in my face when my boss at the magazine added some crap and printed it without the guys even seeing it, which I'd promised them they would." She took another drink of her wine. "During the two weeks I was with them, Noah and I got close, really close. I went back to Los Angeles and when he saw the article, he was so mad, he threatened a lawsuit against me and the magazine." Her gaze focused on the ring on her left ring finger. "We finally got to talk, and he understood it wasn't me that printed the article the way it was."

"You're engaged now?"

"Yes. We haven't set a date, but he did ask me to marry him."

"That's so cool. He seems like a nice guy."

Tori giggled, pressing her fingers to her lips, her eyes alight with mirth. "He can be. He has his moments though, just like any other rock star. They are self-indulgent, conceited, and spoiled, but he's also very loving, patient with me, killer in the sack, and I love him with all my heart."

"I think it is very cool you two are so in love."

"I'd like to kill him at times too."

"How are you going to work it out when they go on the upcoming tour? They have some shows in Europe as well, right?"

With a finger held up, Tori took another drink of her wine, draining the glass. "I'm working remotely with Lyric so I can travel with them. I'm not sure how I will do with the women hanging on Noah all the time, but I'll learn, I guess. I know he loves me, and I trust him. We'll be okay."

"You haven't had to deal with the ladies throwing themselves at him yet?"

"No. We've been together a short time, really."

"How long?"

"Two months."

Surprised at how quick things moved with them, Maddie asked, "And you're engaged already?"

"Yeah." Tori rolled the engagement ring around her finger. "Noah didn't waste any time." She raised her gaze to Maddie's. "I'm not as confident as I seem. I'm still very nervous and unsure about my relationship. It happened so fast, it was crazy, and now we are going to be traveling all over the place, with women coming onto him and everything. God, I wish we'd had more time to be together before I had to deal with this." Tori held out her glass for another round of the wine.

"I'm sure it will be fine. It's obvious Noah loves you by the way he treats you. He has eyes only for you."

"Do you really think so?"

"I know so. I can see it."

Tori took her hand, squeezing her fingers. "Thank you. You have no idea how hard it is not having someone to talk to about this kind of stuff."

Maddie smiled. Her life revolved around computers and programming. She knew exactly what it felt like to not have anyone to talk to about girl things, guys, and what to do about a certain rock star. The wine went down her throat with a sweet sting, giving her a little fortification to open her mouth. "What do you know about Alex?"

"Are you sure you want to go there? I swear I didn't come over here to talk about him."

Another sip of wine and she said, "Yes. At least I think so."

"I haven't known him long, only since I met the whole band a few months ago, but he seems like he can be really nice on one hand and a bit of a manwhore on the other."

Madison snorted, a deep laugh exploding from her mouth before she could stop it. "That's an understatement."

"You live across from him. You didn't already know him?"

She glanced away, afraid to reveal her stalking tendencies. When she looked back, Tori's eyes were wide with curiosity. "I did sort of. I knew he owned an apartment across from here when I bought this place."

"It's gorgeous, by the way. It must have cost a pretty penny right here on Central Park."

"Thanks and yes. I have a patent on a computer program that I developed. It's made me a lot of money, enough to afford this."

"That's awesome."

"Anyway, yes, I knew who he was before we met downstairs a few days ago. I didn't set it up for my cat to get out and for him to catch him, if that's what you're thinking."

"Nope. Didn't even cross my mind."

"It happened is all."

"Are you attracted to him?"

Madison thought about the way her skin goose bumped when he touched her, how her breath caught when his breath brushed against her ear, and how she'd almost drowned in his sensual assault during dinner. If he hadn't ruined it by pushing too hard, she probably would have given in and went to bed with him. His arrogance was something she had a problem with. "You could say that, yes. I mean, he touches me, the way I react to his nearness—everything has me totally on edge when he's close."

"You've got it bad, girl."

"Maybe, but he's about the most egotistical guy I've ever been around."

"He's a rock star. He doesn't have to work for a woman's attention." Tori leaned in. "Do you want him for more than one or two sexy fuck sessions?"

Did she? Oh hell yeah, she did.

Madison nodded. "What do I need to do?"

"We've got this, girlfriend. Men want what they can't have, it is a given, so we don't give him what he wants. Make him work for it. If he has to chase you, it makes the catch all the sweeter in the end."

"Can you help me?"

"Of course. I have full access to the man, his friends included." Tori tapped her finger to her lips and then grinned. "The guys have a promo session they have to do in two days. It's a big party to promote their new album and the upcoming tour. It's something their manager set up last minute when he heard they'd all be in town this week. Everyone who is anyone will be there." With her lip between her teeth, Tori pointed at Madison.

"Do you have a killer dress? I mean something that will knock his socks off?"

The grin pulling up the corners of Madison's mouth got bigger and bigger as the vision of the perfect dress flashed in her mind. "I don't right now, but I have a credit card and know the perfect store." She climbed to her feet, swaying a little from the wine. "Shall we go shopping?"

Chapter Seven

The roar of the music was deafening as Madison stepped from the cab. The vibration had the windows moving. Even though Tori and Noah had offered to let her ride with them, she didn't want Alex to see her before she made an entrance to the party, and she didn't want to be beholden to them should things go south.

Her heart pounded against her ribs, doing a bongo rhythm she didn't recognize. Maybe she was sick and needed to go home. *Yeah, that's it.* She turned on her high heel, but before she could flag a cab to run screaming back to her apartment, a hand grabbed her arm, spinning her around to face Tori.

"No chickening out." Her gaze raked down the dress Madison had on. "Wow. You look fantastic!"

The dress they'd picked out from a very chic boutique not far from her place was gorgeous. Black lace covered her upper arms to her elbows, leaving her shoulders bare. The sweetheart neckline exposed enough cleavage to make any man drool and with the small pearl drop necklace she had on, the eyes were drawn to her creamy skin. The hem of the dress was short, very short, barely covering her ass cheeks and if she bent over, she'd be flashing everyone and showing them she wore no underwear. Why she'd chosen not to wear any was beyond her. *Tempting one gorgeous rock star comes to mind.* Black four-inch heels made her legs look killer. "Thanks, but I think this is a big mistake. What if Alex doesn't even notice me?"

The snort Tori released made Madison smile even through the sick feeling in her stomach. "Oh, he'll notice you, all right. He won't be able to keep his eyes or his hands off you, but you have to be strong. No giving in to his baser wants, even if they are the same as yours."

Madison forced a breath from her lungs as she smoothed her hand over her hip. "Let's go then."

The thumping of the bass made her chest quiver with each beat. It was a weird sensation. A large crowd rolled in the center, bumping and grinding together as if they couldn't stop touching each other. Stopping to watch for a second left her hot, horny, and a whole lot needy. Lights flashed, colors whirled, and she wondered if they would even be able to find the guys in the huge room. Her gaze moved from one side to the other, taking it all in, impressed with the number of people gathered on such short notice. It was New York after all and parties were well attended.

Tori took her hand, guiding her along until the sea of bodies parted revealing the guys in the band huddled together at a large table near the front of the room, stacks of posters, CD's, and t-shirts at their fingertips. Several big guys stood at each end of the table, apparently to keep the overzealous fans at bay.

"Oh my God!" A blonde with huge boobs stood in front of the table, taking her turn with each guy. "I absolutely love you." She leaned over the table, wrapping her arms around Noah's neck and trying to plant her lips on his.

Madison heard Tori growl next to her, but before she could lunge, Maddie placed a hand on her arm as the bouncer grabbed the girl and peeled her off Noah.

"Too close, ma'am."

"What? No! I've waited for over a year to get this close to Iron Rogue. I've bought all of their music. I've been to eight of their shows. The least I can get is a kiss."

Tori plastered a smile on her lips and moved next to the girl where she stood with her upper arm clasped in the large fist of the bouncer. "Bitch, if you touch my man again, I will deflate those boobs of yours and feed them to you one small silicone piece at a time."

The girl turned toward her with her mouth open and then closed it quickly before yanking her arm out of the bouncers grasp and disappearing into the crowd.

Noah nodded to the guy and then after the girl, giving him the clear instruction to make sure the woman didn't return. The huge man said something into the microphone, clipped to his lapel, which Maddie hadn't seen before, and then took his place again.

Tori grinned as she moved behind Noah and placed her hand on his shoulder, engagement ring flashing in the light. The girl knew how to stake her claim as Noah grasped her fingers and kissed them.

Madison had stayed behind a few others, not wanting Alex to see her until she felt ready, if she ever felt ready. How would he react? Would he even notice her at all in this massive crowd of beautiful people? She wasn't anything special, a computer nerd playing dress up and totally out of her element.

The group shifted, revealing Alex in all his gorgeous self. His head was bent as he signed a photo and shoved it down the table toward Aiden before he looked up. His gaze locked on hers, and a slow appreciative grin lifted the corners of his mouth as he climbed to his feet. The pen he'd been using to sign dropped to the table with a soundless bounce.

Unable to move or even breathe, Madison stood stock still when Alex moved around the table and came to a stop in front of her. His gaze did a slow crawl down her body and then back up again before he leaned in. "Hey, gorgeous."

"Hey yourself," she breathed.

"I'm glad you came."

"Are you?" she asked, afraid of his answer.

He tucked her against his side and led her around the table to where his chair sat vacant. "I would have invited you myself, but I thought you were still mad at me."

"I am." She touched his jaw with her fingertips. "We can talk about that later."

He glanced at the watch on his wrist. "We have about an hour to go on this meet and greet, then I'll be able to give you my full attention."

"I'd like that."

A chair appeared nearby. "Sit here and make all the women jealous."

Once he took his chair, the procession continued with probably over five hundred people filing through the line. Each one of them took pictures, signed autographs, gave away music, posters, and t-shirts galore, all in the name of promotion. Listening to the music playing in the background, Madison realized the songs were Iron Rogue's and it had to be their new CD. She listened carefully to Noah's voice as he sang each one, some raw and rough and some soft and romantic. Madison paid closer attention to those in the room, noticing many were dressed in suits with pretty women on their arms, talking amongst themselves for several moments before they would pay attention to the band.

Alex leaned back toward her chair during a break in the crowd. "Record people. Promotion VIPs. Fans." He nodded to a portly man standing a few feet away. "Bigwig from our label. He's checking us out to make sure we're making them enough money." Another tip of his head toward a leggy brunette. "She's a huge promoter. She pushes our music and tour dates to the venues we book all over the country." His eyes glittered when they set on Madison. "She's got the hots for Aiden, but he won't give her the time of day. His heart is still set on a girl from high school."

Madison glanced at Aiden who talked with Dylan next to him. "That's sad."

"Not really. He's being stubborn and won't contact her, even though he won't get serious with anyone else."

A teenage boy came down the line, stopping to talk to Noah for a moment before he moved on and stood in front of Alex, holding out a guitar. "Would you sign this for me, Mr. Rockly?"

"Sure and it's Alex, okay?"

"Really?"

"Yeah. What's your name buddy?"

"Jamie."

"Do you play, Jamie?"

"Yes, sir."

"Lead or acoustic?"

"Only this for now, but I am saving my money for an electric guitar. I want to be able to play like you."

Madison teared up. *Wow*. Alex probably felt that way when he was a teenager.

"How much do you have so far?"

"I've saved about a hundred bucks. I work with my dad in his garage on weekends."

For several long moments, Alex stared at the kid. He touched his fingers to a scar on his hand and then raised his palm to the burly guy behind him. He whispered something to the man, and the guy disappeared.

"That's awesome. Did you get a poster?"

"Yep and I appreciate it. I love your music, all of you guys. You're my favorite band in the whole world."

"Thanks, buddy."

The bouncer appeared a second later carrying a guitar case, putting it on the floor next to Alex's chair.

"Jamie, what grade are you in school?"

"Tenth. I'm a sophomore."

"So you have two more years to go before you graduate."

"Yeah, but I don't know if I will or not. My grades aren't the greatest and I just want to play music."

Alex stood and moved around the table to stop next to the kid. The music had been silenced for a moment as the crowd moved in. "Listen to me. Graduating is one of the most important things you can do for yourself. Music is a fickle woman. She can be the best lover in the world and then leave you wanting what you can't have. You can be on top of the world one minute and the next be sitting on the street corner trying to peddle CDs."

"I know, but—"

With his hand outstretched, Alex tipped his head to the bouncer and the guy handed him the guitar case. Opening the lid on the top of the table, the crowd gathering around him didn't seem to faze him. "I'll make you a deal, Jamie. You finish high school with a B average—and I'm going to be in touch with your dad to make sure you do—and I will give you this Gibson. You can take it home, but if your grades drop, your dad will be in contact with me."

The boy's face lost all color. "You're giving me your guitar?"

"Yes."

Jamie's hand went out, shaking as he ran his fingertips over the strings on the face. "I don't understand. It's your guitar."

"Buddy, I can buy more if I need to." Alex wrapped his arm around the kid's shoulders.

A tear slipped down Madison's cheek at the gesture this icon, this rock of a man, was doing for this kid.

"I will do everything you said, Alex. I will get the grades and graduate so I can show the world I'm a smart guy, like you." Jamie grabbed Alex in a hug. "I will make you proud of me, I swear."

Alex hugged him back. "You do it for you, Jamie, not for me. You need to be smart about life. No drugs. No messing around. Study hard. Be proud of who you are."

"God. You're the best!" Jamie hugged him again as the bouncer put the lid back on the base and stood it upright. The kid glanced at Madison sitting behind the table. "Is that your lady? She's pretty."

Alex leaned in and whispered something in Jamie's ear. They hugged again before Alex handed him the case and Jamie moved on down the table. Alex returned to his side of the table.

"I can't believe you did that. You probably changed his life."

"I hope so. If it takes nothing more than a guitar to show him he can be whatever he wants, then I would do it for a hundred kids. He seemed special. Reminded me a lot of me when I was sixteen and trying to figure out what to do with my life."

Her heart did a little flip in her chest. The man became six hundred times sexier in that few minutes, and if she wasn't careful falling in love with him wouldn't be hard at all. Heartbreak would be in her future.

* * * *

Nerves had Alex's leg jumping under the cover of the tablecloth. He'd never been nervous in his life, not when he got up to play his guitar for the first time in front of a crowd of people, not when he'd made love to a girl for the first time, and not when he'd seen Madison walk into that room with the killer black dress on. Time was not on his side as he checked his watch for the umpteenth time in the last ten minutes. The scheduled time for their autograph session was almost over and he'd have a chance to hold the woman sitting just behind him, in his arms for the first time tonight. If he didn't touch her soon, he was going to lose his mind.

The second she'd met his gaze tonight, he'd been so fucking hard, he'd hadn't been able to concentrate on a damn word anyone was saying. Pale skin peeked out from beneath the hem of her dress, taunting him to run his fingers up the silky thigh until he reached the promises of what lie beneath. Legs that went on forever, a waist meant for his hands, breasts that were playing peek-a-boo with him every time she moved, and desire burning in her eyes had him ready to throw her over his shoulder and sprint for the door.

He reached back, running the tips of his fingers over her ankle where it sat next to the leg of his chair. A little thrill went through him when she shivered under his touch. She couldn't deny her desire for him, not when her body reacted so strongly to his nearness.

Rick stopped to talk to each of them, giving them the go-ahead to break and mingle with the guests. Alex had no intention of mingling. He wanted to be alone with Madison.

With Maddie's hand in his, he said, "Let's go."

"Where?"

"I don't care. I want you alone."

Her steps stuttered to a stop. "I want to dance, Alex, and your manager said you needed to schmooze with your fans before you take off."

"Fine," he replied, pulling her tight against his chest and wrapping his arms around her so his hands rested on her ass. Her body pressed to his was a bad, very bad idea. Touching the curve of her ass, he sucked in a ragged breath. "You naughty, naughty girl."

She glanced up through her lashes, innocence written all over her face. "Me?"

"You aren't wearing underwear."

"I have no idea what you mean, Alex."

He pressed a kiss to the spot beneath her earlobe as he whispered, "Temptress." The seduction of Madison Avery had begun.

"Alex, I need you to meet someone," Rick said, tapping him on the back.

"Now?"

"Yeah."

Never one to let a good thing get away, Alex tucked Madison against his side, his hand possessively on her hip. Rick led him across the room toward a group of men standing near the back.

Introductions were made, with most of the names and faces not even registering in Alex's brain, only the curve of the hip under his fingertips made an impact on his synapses. Even the men had eyes only for Madison, drawing out possessiveness on his part. He didn't want anyone to look at the gorgeous woman next to him, except him. She was his, damn it.

Olive skinned, dark eyes, and obviously wealthy, one of the men in the group stepped forward to take Madison's hand in what Alex thought to be an all too familiar grasp. "'Who might this lovely lady be?"

Alex felt a feral growl rumbling in his throat. "Madison Avery. A *very* close friend of mine."

"Nice to meet you," she replied, holding the man's hand a little longer than necessary.

"It was great chatting with you, gentleman, but we need to make the rounds of the room. If you'll excuse us." Alex pulled Madison away with a firm grip on her hip, effectively removing her but keeping her at his side.

"That was kind of rude, Alex. They were people you probably needed to talk to if they had something to do with your tour or records."

"They aren't anything other than obnoxious investors who want a piece of us. Don't worry your gorgeous head over them," he said, pulling her back onto the dance floor as a slow song began and he could have her in his arms again. "You smell fucking fantastic."

"Are you trying to seduce me?" she asked, her voice breathless and warm against his neck.

"Is it working because I'm about to lose my mind for wanting you beneath me."

"Maybe."

"I need you, Maddie, more than my next breath."

"I'm sure that's the same line you use on every woman you want, Alex."

He stared down into her eyes, trying desperately to figure out what was so different about her that he couldn't think beyond having her. "Why is it the one woman I want more than anything in the world, is the one woman who is resisting me at every turn?"

"I don't know what you mean."

He grabbed her hand before nodding to Noah and almost caveman dragging her out the door of the hotel. Unable to keep himself at bay, he pushed her against the wall, his mouth taking hers in a bruising kiss. "I'm taking you home."

"Good idea," she said breathlessly.

Alex practically shoved Maddie through the door of a cab waiting at the curb, door open, engine running, her dress riding her thighs like he wanted to with his hands.

After rattling off the address, he almost shouted at the driver. "Move."

"Yes, sir."

The cab zigzagged through traffic, throwing Maddie against his side. "Easy, babe. I've got you."

He grabbed the hairs at the back of her head, tipping it back so he could take her mouth. Tongues lashed, breaths mingled, and his head swam with need for this woman. Tonight she would be his.

A screech indicated they were at the apartment complex.

He flung open the door, taking Maddie's hand to pull her to his side. She wobbled on her heels for a second. He bent down and quickly removed them from her feet, sweeping her up in his arms.

"Alex?"

Holy hell, he couldn't wait to get her alone. "Yeah?"

"My apartment."

He nodded, throwing some money at the driver before rushing them across the street, up the elevator, never once leaving her mouth for more than a few seconds.

The moment they reached her floor, the doors slid open, and he let her slide down his body so she could get her keys.

Her phone jingled in her purse.

Her gaze met his and for the love of all that was Holy, he knew he was screwed and not in a good way.

Son of a bitch.

Chapter Eight

Madison sighed as she leaned back against the door of her apartment. She'd managed to keep Alex at bay and even made it home without letting him between her thighs, one thing she wanted more than anything in this world.

Her cell phone rang again, and she fumbled for it as she headed to her bedroom to bang her head against the wall for telling him no.

"You didn't sleep with him, did you?"

"Hello, Tori, and no, he left with nothing more than a kiss, which by the way, left me drooling and horny as hell."

"Good. Now we move onto plan B."

"Plan B?"

"Yep."

Her phone beeped in her ear. "Hang on. I have another call." She clicked over and said, "Hello?"

"Hey, babe. It's Alex."

"Hi." She frowned. "How did you get my number?"

"Tori."

"I see." She blew out a breath. "Remind me to chew her out, would you please?"

"Don't do that. I bribed her."

"With what?"

"Chocolate. I know she'd do almost anything for chocolate and there is a killer shop down the street."

"Yes, I know. The Chocolate Factory."

"That's the one!"

"It's one of my favorite places to go."

"I'll remember that." He paused for a second and then said, "I have a question for you."

"Okay. Shoot."

"I would like to take you out to dinner and a show tomorrow night. Can you make it?"

She wasn't sure what to say for a moment. *Breathe. Breathe.* "Like on a date?" He laughed, and she felt like smacking him through the phone.

"Yes, Madison. A date. I'll pick you up at six. We'll have dinner, go to a Broadway show if you'd like, and see where things go from there."

A chill raced down her spine. A date with Alex? Wasn't that in the direction she wanted to go? She'd played hard to get until her thighs were a quivering mass of needy flesh, aching to have him between them. Her heart hammered in her chest. Should she say yes?

"Madison?"

"I guess that would be all right."

"Great. I'll see you at six tomorrow then. You can wear that dress you wore tonight. You looked like a million bucks in it."

"Thank you."

"See you then."

She ended the call and pressed her phone to her chest a second before it beeped in her hand, making her realize Tori was still on the other line. "Oh my God. I'm so sorry."

"It's okay. Alex, right?"

"How'd you know? And by the way, I should kill you for giving him my number."

Tori laughed on the other end of the line. "Isn't that what you wanted? For him to chase you?"

"Well, yes, but—"

"Besides, he offered chocolate if I told. I couldn't very well resist that, now could I?"

"I guess not, but if this doesn't work and he doesn't fall in love with me, I will personally kill you with my bare hands."

"Yeah, yeah," Tori said something to Noah before coming back to the line. "So? What did he want?"

Madison unzipped her dress, letting it fall to her feet. "He asked me out on a date tomorrow night. Dinner and a Broadway show." Her bra came next, falling to the floor in a puddle of black lace. Just as Alex knew, she hadn't worn underwear simply to drive him wild.

"A date?"

"Yeah."

"Alex never dates, and I mean never according to Noah." She giggled. "This is good, really good."

Soft flannel slipped down her body in a cuddly glide of material. "I hope you're right about this."

"I am. Trust me."

"Exactly when do I get to have wild, wall-banging sex with him, because I'm about to lose my mind over here." She pulled the curtain back half an inch, peeking through to see if she could spot anything going on in his apartment. The lights were on, but she couldn't see any movement. "You don't understand how long it has been since I've had good sex, not even great sex, but good sex. I'd settle for that."

"If all goes as planned, I'd say by the end of next week."

"What the fuck, Tori? End of next week? My dildo won't last that long. I have already went through three sets of batteries in the last two days."

"Easy, girl. It'll be okay. By the time you two do the dirty, he'll be eating out of your hand and ready to put a ring on it."

Madison blew out a long breath. "Do I have to remind you if this doesn't work, I will kill you in your sleep?"

"Bye, Maddie. I'll talk to you tomorrow."

Yanking open her top nightstand drawer, Madison pulled out her toy and parked her butt on the edge of the bed. She needed sex. She needed Alex.

It was going to be a long night.

* * * *

Five thirty the next evening, Madison stood in front of her mirror dabbing at her nose trying desperately to stop the run of snot down her face. A sneeze spread clear liquid all over her mirror. "Fucking hell to the no."

Her cheeks were pink with fever, and her stomach rolled from nausea. This wasn't good. She was supposed to be ready to meet Alex in thirty minutes. A date wouldn't be possible tonight.

"I never go out. The one night I go to a party and what happens? I get sick, not a little sick, but snot running, nose blowing, fever-inducing sick!"

She grabbed her cell phone and dialed Tori's number.

"Hey, girl. Are you ready for your date?"

Her nose was so stopped up, she couldn't breathe. "No." Her head felt like it was about to implode, squashing her brain with the amount of snot no normal person should ever have.

"What the hell? Are you sick, Maddie?"

"Yes." Her voice sounded like a remake of the Terminator including the gravelly voice of Arnold Schwarzenegger. "I knew I shouldn't have gone to that party." A loud sneeze echoed in her head as she moaned. "My head hurts."

"Oh, honey. I'm so sorry."

"This is why I don't go out." She sneezed again. "I can't go on a date like this, Tori."

"What time is he going to be there?"

Madison looked at the clock on the wall. "In ten minutes." A knock sounded at the door. "Or now."

"Answer it."

"I can't!"

"Yes, you can. He'll understand. Trust me on this."

She walked to the door with a tissue up her nose to stop the snot from running down her face and looked through the peephole. It was Alex.

He knocked again.

Unable to keep from groaning as she turned her head to whisper in the phone. "I'll talk to you later."

"Madison?" He knocked a little louder. "Babe, are you in there?"

Closing her eyes, she prayed for a little help and opened the door.

"Holy shit, Maddie. You look like hell, sweetheart." He moved inside and shut the door behind him. "What happened?"

"I have a cold."

He touched her forehead. "I can see that. You're also running a fever."

His arm around her, he lead her back into the bedroom, tucked her under the warm blankets, and then pulled up a chair beside her bed.

"I'm sorry, Alex."

"For what?"

"I ruined our date."

"Baby, there will be other dates." He ran his fingers down her cheek. "Have you been like this all day?"

She nodded and rubbed her finger under her nose. "Since early this morning. It woke me up."

He pushed her sticky hair off her forehead. "Did you take anything?"

A shake of her head was the answer.

"Do you have anything here to take?"

Again, she shook her head.

"I'll be right back." He kissed the top of her head. "Don't move."

About twenty minutes later, Alex returned with a huge bag in his hands. He handed her a box of super soft Kleenex, a glass of water, and two pills.

"These are for your head, but they also have Tylenol in them for the fever."

She struggled to sit up, so he put his arm behind her shoulders and lifted her, giving her the chance to swallow the medication before lying back against the pillows.

"I wish you would have called me."

"I didn't want to bother you."

The tsking sound he gave her made her smile, even though her head pounded like someone was inside with a sledgehammer.

"I'll be right back."

He disappeared out the door for several minutes, only to return with a bowl sitting on a plate in his hands along with a glass of something bubbly.

"My mother always said chicken soup was good for colds and whatever else ails you." He handed her the plate and then put the glass on the table. "Ginger Ale. It helps settle the stomach." He went back out into the living room for a moment, returning with a teddy bear bigger than anything she'd ever seen. "This is to keep you company when I'm not here."

"Aw." She looked up into his eyes, realizing this was an Alex she hadn't know existed. "Thank you. He's adorable." This couldn't be real, could it?

He tucked the bear next to her on the bed. "There. Now you won't be lonely."

Not sure how to respond, she slowly ate her soup, eyeing him the whole time although he didn't seem to notice at all. He talked about the plans for the band, his house in Iowa, growing up a farm kid in the middle of the cornfields, and how the band came to exist. Some of the things he mentioned, she already knew, but it was interesting to hear him tell it from his perspective.

Her head began to clear a little, the pain receding to a dull ache between her eyes. The snot didn't seem to be trying to drown her anymore, and the sneezing had subsided a bit.

Alex touched her forehead. "Your fever seems to be down. Are you feeling better?"

"A little." She picked at the blanket lying across her abdomen. "Thank you for taking care of me. I probably would have been found in my bathroom in a few days, dead from snot overload."

A smile graced his lips. "As long as this wasn't a ploy to get out of our date."

Shocked he would even think a thing, she said, "Oh no. Of course not. I was looking forward to it."

His fingers reached for her face, tucking a stray piece of hair behind her ear. "Good."

A huge yawn made her jaw pop. "Wow. I'm so sorry. The warm soup and everything has made me sleepy."

Climbing to his feet, he leaned in and touched his lips to her cheek. "Then sleep, beautiful. I'll talk to you tomorrow morning to see how you're feeling."

Her eyes were heavy, but she didn't want him to go. "Stay. Please?"

"Are you sure?"

"Yes."

He toed off his shoes, removed his jacket, and climbed into the bed next to her after moving Buddy the Bear to the rocking chair in the corner. With his arm around her shoulders, she tucked her head against his chest, his chin resting on top of her head, and eased into the best sleep she'd had in a very long time.

The warmth of something beneath her cheek woke Madison. Darkness surrounded her so she couldn't really see what was going on, but the rise and fall of the hard surface confused her. Vague images of Alex coming to her apartment rushed across her mind until she realized they were accurate and the sexy smell reaching her nose was the man she couldn't seem to forget.

"How are you feeling?" he asked, his voice low and raspy.

Goosebumps raced across her arms. "Better." Her head didn't feel as full and she could actually breathe a little through her nose. She glanced up from his chest, still unable to make out his features. His hair tickled her arm and shoulder where it laid over her skin.

The clock on the bedside table read two a.m. when she eased up to see the numbers.

"You probably need more medication before the other dose totally wears off and you are all full of snot again."

"Okay."

He eased out from under her, taking his warmth and comfort with him. Once he had the glass in his hand, he walked barefoot into the bathroom to retrieve more water and medication. "Here. Take these." Two pills were handed to her along with the glass.

After she swallowed them down, she said, "You don't have to take care of me, Alex. I think I'm over the worst of it. Thank you, though. You've been a lifesaver."

"Are you kicking me out, Maddie? Because I kind of like holding you while you slept."

"N-no. I mean, you can stay if you want."

"Good." He slid back onto the bed, pulled her against his side, and let out a big sigh. "Lie down and sleep now. You'll need your rest for tomorrow."

"I do?" she whispered.

"Yes. We have a date to make up for."

"Alex?"

"Yeah?"

"You're a great friend."

* * * *

A great friend. Damn it! That's the last fucking thing I want to be, but I guess I'll take what I can get at the moment.

Her breathing eased into an even in and out rhythm telling him she slept again. Good. She needed it to get over this crud, whatever it was. He prayed he didn't catch it being this close to her. Giving this up wasn't an option though.

He let his fingers do a slow crawl up and down her arm, loving the feel of her silky skin beneath the pads on his fingertips. Not sure why she held such fascination for him, he peeked down at where she lie across his chest and smiled. He couldn't remember the last time he'd been in bed with a woman like this. It was different. The closeness with her went beyond what he had ever felt for anyone. *But relationships aren't my thing, not now, not ever.* His gaze narrowed as he focused on the light coming through the window from somewhere outside.

Contemplation didn't come easy for him. He didn't do it often, and when he did, things never made much sense. The mystery of the universe still held him spellbound. It was okay, since even the smartest of men had no idea what any of it meant.

The only thing he knew for certain was the band meant everything to him. His parents had divorced when he was younger and the guitar had been his outlet. With his father only around on occasion, he'd done a lot of shitty things, stealing, drugs, run-ins with the law, but when he'd found the guitar, his whole life had become focused on that. Guitar riffs were his way of communicating his feelings, opening up to the possibilities of what life had to offer. No one had ever come close to becoming that for him. The run in with his dad the day the band finished their signature song had been a changing point. He'd locked himself away from them, turning his back on his biological family for the most part. His parents had stayed close after their divorce, even reconciling after the kids had grown and left the house. They'd remarried a few years ago.

A sigh escaped Madison's lips as she rubbed her cheek against his chest in her sleep. It didn't matter that he barely knew her, she'd held him spellbound since the moment they'd met. Normally, he could barely remember a woman's name after sex, much less anything else about her. With this one, he couldn't seem to forget her, and they hadn't even had sex yet. That was a first for him.

His eyes felt heavy with sleep. He hadn't slept much the night before, thinking about Madison and her gorgeous body. When she'd turned him away at the door of her apartment, he had to admit, he'd been pissed off and horny. Good Lord was he horny. All of her creamy skin visible through the slits of her dress, made his body crave only her. Her eyes told him she wanted him too, but for some reason, she was denying them both.

The minute she'd gotten over this snot inducing infection, he would have her, all of her, and they wouldn't be leaving her apartment or his, he didn't care which, until they were both well satisfied.

It might take several days.

Alex awoke the next morning to running water, the sounds of the shower, and an empty bed. Wads of Kleenex lay everywhere, on the bed, on the dresser, on the nightstand, and on the floor. He couldn't help smiling. If Madison was in the shower, she felt better.

Tossing his legs over the side of the bed, he decided then and there, Madison Avery would be his before the day ended.

The door to the bathroom opened silently under his hand, revealing the fogged up shower stall with the fuzzy outline of the most beautiful woman he'd ever laid eyes on. Her breasts were high and full. Her hips were curvy, just enough for him to hold onto, and her legs were long and lean, perfect to wrap around his hips. His palms itched to touch all of that skin.

"Alex?"

He cleared his throat, knowing desire clogged his brain for a moment. "Yeah."

Silence kept him still near the door.

"Care to join me?"

He'd never stripped so fast in his life.

Naked as the day he was born, he pulled open the shower door only to find Madison standing under the spray, hair slicked back with water and the most gorgeous smile on her face.

The sigh rushing from his lips made him realize he'd been holding his breath, anticipation raw in his gut.

"Hi," she said, dropping her gaze down his chest only to stop on his cock. "Happy to see me?"

"You have no idea, babe." His hand shook as he reached out to touch her shoulder, smoothing over the skin from her collarbone to her biceps, enjoying every inch under his hand. "I've waited for this for days."

"Not days?"

His gaze found hers, loving the brightness of her eyes as her lips tilted up in a smile.

"Maybe even weeks." *Maybe a lifetime.* "Are you sure about this?"

"I've never been more sure of anything in my life."

She wrapped her hand around his cock, driving him insane with lust. He tipped his head back, releasing a long groan of desire he couldn't hold in. "Easy. It's been a while."

"How long exactly, Alex?"

He placed open-mouth kisses along her shoulder, tracing her collarbone with his tongue. "You wouldn't believe me if I told you."

Her head moved so he could get better access to that sweet spot below her ear.

"Sure I would," she whispered, her body shivering under his touch.

"Six months."

She went completely still for several moments. "Really?"

"Yeah."

She looked up into his eyes. "Why?"

He brushed his lips against her jawline, slowly working his way to her mouth. "I've been waiting for you."

Chapter Nine

Everything stopped for that brief moment when his words sank in. He'd been waiting for her? In that moment, her heart became wholly, undoubtedly his. Her thoughts whirled around in her head, disjointed yet focused on those five words.

His lips brushed hers in a sensual slide as every emotion slammed into her at once. She needed this man more than her next breath, and she didn't care if they had a future, she didn't care if it would be a short interlude and her heart was broken in the end, she wanted this.

Her hands wandered up his chest, feeling each muscle under her palms, enjoying the hard plains beneath her fingertips. His body was ripped, every dip and valley giving her pleasure as she explored.

He deepened the kiss, devouring her mouth, taking his pleasure with a brush of his tongue against hers, pushing her to succumb to his wants like someone starved for water in the hot desert sun. His hands moved over her shoulders, learning her curves like a blind man.

His lips left hers only to travel along her cheek, jawline, and then her neck with a sexy nip every few inches.

One hand on her hip kept her in place, not that she had anywhere else she'd rather be but right there. The other hand cupped her breast and kneaded the soft flesh before pinching her nipple between his finger and thumb, dragging a needy moan from her mouth. The wet sensation of his lips enveloping the tip forced that moan into a breathless sigh of his name. "Alex."

The water began to cool.

Leaving her for a brief second, he grabbed a towel from the rack outside the shower door and held it open for her to step inside. "Let's take this back into the other room, shall we? The first time I make love to you, I want it to be everything you've ever thought making love could be. Your pleasure is mine."

The warm towel heated her skin, scratching the oversensitive surface with a sensually erotic sensation.

His lips did a slow crawl over her shoulder as he rubbed her skin dry before using it quickly to blot the wetness from his own.

He took her hand, leading her back into the bedroom until they stood at the side of the bed. His gaze raked her body with an intense stare, taking in everything until it returned to her eyes. "You are the most beautiful woman I have ever had the pleasure to touch."

"I bet that's not true, but thank you."

A frown pulled at the corners of his lips. "You don't believe you are beautiful?"

"I know I'm pretty plain next to the women you're normally with. I love that you think I could compare to them."

"Madison." His hand stopped at her hips. "You have soft curves, hips made for my hands, breasts that most woman would die for and pay highly for." He brought one finger up to trace her lips. "You have a killer mouth, one I can't wait to see wrapped around my cock at some point." His hand moved behind her head to cup her neck, bringing her closer still. "Your lips taste fantastic, and I can't stop kissing you." Several small nips at the corners of her mouth made her smile seconds before he kissed her, taking her mouth in a soul-shattering mating she wouldn't be able to repeat with anyone else in this lifetime or any other.

Experience had to count for something because the man had more than his share of talent. Every brush of his tongue against hers, every moan of desire, and every touch of his fingers brought her higher than she'd been before.

He traced the curve of her breast, until he held the weight in his palm, and let his thumb trace the areola around and around before he finally pinched her nipple between his thumb and first finger. A desperate moan escaped her as he moved down her neck like a man on a mission.

The second his lips encircled her nipple, she felt like she'd died and gone to heaven. Her body hummed with desire, need racing along her nerves until she thought she'd go mad if he didn't do something to quell the burning, achy tightness between her thighs. "Alex, please."

"Ah, sweet girl. I'll take care of you. I promise."

Fingers dipped between her legs, the calluses on the pads abrading deliciously against her clit. Everything narrowed into one sensation. Her body trembled as her desire rose to impossible proportions, taking her along the path to ultimate mind-blowing need so strong she thought she'd lose her mind.

Whimpers escaped her lips. If he didn't make her come soon, she would have to punch him.

He smiled against her skin, and she knew he was fully aware of what he was doing to her.

"Easy, baby."

Easing her down, he followed her with open-mouthed kisses between her breasts, until she lay flat on her back, him on top of her.

Alex trailed his lips down her body, stopping every few seconds to nip at her skin, leaving little love bites along the way, until he reached his goal.

He kissed his way up from her ankle, nibbling at the back of her knees. Parting her thighs with his shoulders, he pressed his lips to the inside of each leg. Sliding his tongue along her skin, he left goosebumps in his wake as he got closer still to the place she needed him the most.

Her breath held—waiting.

The moment he brushed the tip of his tongue over her clit, her world exploded into a thousand shards of light raining down on her. He continued to lick and suck on her until she thought she'd go crazy with orgasm after orgasm flooding her system, dragging her into a void where nothing existed except Alex.

Ragged breath sawed in and out of her mouth as she tried to catch what was left of her brain cells.

When he moved up her body, the tickle of his hair along her legs made her giggle.

"You are not doing my ego any good by laughing while I'm supposed to be making your eyes roll back in your head." His lips brushed over her nipple, his tongue raking a path from one to the other.

A small bite to the tip bowed her back with the sting, dragging a long moan from her mouth.

"Now there is a sound I like," he whispered along her neck.

One hand reached out to the bedside where he'd placed his wallet.

Cool latex brushed the inside of her thigh a moment later, making her realize he'd put a condom on to protect them both. The man was gorgeous *and* smart.

In no hurry to bring things to a conclusion, Madison let her fingers roam over his biceps, down his arms to his hands, and up over his muscled back, before tracing down until she could reach his butt. The man had a body most guys would love to have and every woman wanted, including her.

He began his assault on her senses again, bringing her up until her body hummed and blood rushed in her ears.

Leaving trails of scratches down his back from her fingernails, she pleaded, "God, Alex, please. I need you."

The head of his cock pushed into her entrance, forcing her to hold her breath at the sensation. *Full, so full.* Perfect.

His breathing became ragged as he held his position for a moment.

"You okay?"

"Yeah." He opened his eyes and put his forehead against hers. "Trying to hold my shit together so this isn't over too soon.

You feel so good, I'm desperately trying not to blow before we're ready."

The gentle, slow glide of his cock into her pussy was the absolute best feeling. With her legs wrapped around his hips, he pushed all the way in until his balls rested against her ass. The man wasn't huge, but he fit just right.

"Holy shit," he breathed. "You're fantastic."

She couldn't help smiling. Alex Rockly was making love to her, he'd said it himself.

As his hips began a slow rocking motion, his lips nipped at her jawline, her neck, and her ears before coming back to take her mouth. His tongue danced with hers, tangling, and loving each other until his movements sped up.

He tore his lips from hers to hold her hips with one hand and lift his chest from hers with the other as he began to pound into her with a fevered rhythm meant to bring them both to a mind-blowing orgasm. He wasn't going to stop until she had one.

Sweat clung to his upper lip. Another bead making its way from his temple. His concentration apparent with his eyes scrunched shut, his mouth set in a line, and his jaw working overtime as it jumped under the skin.

Her hands were braced on the headboard, holding herself in place while he fucked her senseless, her body reacting to his on the most visceral level she could ever have imagined.

His eyes opened, focusing on her face as a little grin lifted the corners of his mouth. "Come with me, Maddie."

Everything exploded inside her, her pussy taking everything he had with each thrust of his hips until he lost control himself. Shuddering above her, he spilling his cum into the end of the condom before he eased himself down on top of her. His warm breath flittered along her neck as she gently ran her hands along his back.

Morning after or whatever you wanted to call this, was always the awkward part for Madison. She didn't know whether to hold him, kiss him, or let him go. Limited experience with this part of things left her confused. Rock stars weren't known for cuddling after sex.

Alex rolled off her, pulling her with him until she lay sprawled across his chest.

That answers that question, I guess.

She peeked up through her lashes at his face. His arm was slung across his eyes, his hair was a tangled sexy mess, and a small smile played on his mouth.

"Done looking?"

"Nope. You're gorgeous post-sex."

One eye appeared below his arm. "And I love that flushed look on your cheeks from my whiskers."

She touched her face, realizing her skin was hot.

"You're beautiful," he said, running his fingers over her lips. "I could stare at you all day."

His cell phone rang next to his wallet on the bedside table. After a low grumble, he grabbed it and brought it to his ear. "What's up, Aiden?"

Maddie could hear some of the conversation even though Alex had it tight against his ear.

"Dylan? What's wrong with him?"

A murmur, but no discernible words came across to her, but Alex sounded worried.

"I'll be there in a few minutes. Don't let him go anywhere."

Alex hung up before releasing a long sigh.

"Fun time is over, babe. I gotta go." He wiggled out from under her and slung his legs over the side of the bed.

"Everything okay?"

"No. I'm not sure what's going on, but I need to help the guys." He pulled on his suit pants and dress shirt. "I'm sorry. I don't want to leave like this."

She got up on her knees on the bed, pulling the sheet up around her bare breasts. "It's okay. I understand." After she raked her fingers through her short hair, she added, "I have work to get done anyway since I was sick yesterday. I'm behind on a deadline."

Alex's gaze held something, she wasn't sure exactly what, but a strange look passed over his face and then was gone. "All right. I'll call you later."

He gently shut the door behind him as Madison sat down with her back to the headboard contemplating what just happened. The front door shut a few moments later, making her realize he was gone.

Now what?

* * * *

Alex made it back to his apartment before he lost his shit. Dylan got drunk last night, stole a car, and then barreled into a tree. He was now in the emergency room at one of the hospitals. *I am going to fucking kill him!* His stupid friend would probably end up in jail and the tour would go to hell.

Throwing on some jeans, a t-shirt, and a pair of boots, Alex grabbed his car keys and headed for the hospital. This shit had to stop. He had no idea what Dylan was going through, but now he was putting all their lives in jeopardy with his antics.

The minute he sprinted through the hospital room doors, he found Noah, Tori, and Aiden sitting in the waiting room with a horde of reporters just outside the glass enclosure being kept at bay by security. Alex tipped his chin as he approached them. "What's the word?"

Noah rose to his feet to pace, running his hands through his long black hair. "He's still unconscious. All we know is he's in pretty bad shape, Alex." Noah stopped and turned toward him. "Do you have any idea what the hell is going on with him?"

Alex took a seat next to Aiden, dropping his hands between his knees as he looked up at one of his best friends. "I don't, Noah. He hasn't mentioned anything to me. Hell, he just showed up here a few days ago, right before you guys. He didn't warn me or anything, only a call when he got here." Alex rubbed his hands along the thigh of his jeans. "He's been kind of bummed out lately, you know, stressed. I don't know why though."

Noah looked at Aiden. "Anything from you?"

Aiden shook his head and said, "Nope. Nothing."

Their manager came through the doors a few minutes later. "Any word?"

"No," Noah replied. "Did you bring security so the hospital doesn't have to deal with these reporters?"

"Yeah. The guys are out there getting the rundown now. I'm sure the hospital will be glad to be relieved."

Taylor came sliding in on her boot heels. "What's going on? Where's Dylan?"

Noah took her by the hand and put her in a chair before kneeling down in front of her. "He's been hurt, Taylor. He's unconscious right now, but the doctors are sure he'll be okay from what they can tell."

A woman in a long white lab coat and a pair of blue scrubs came into the room. "Are you all with Dylan Mannix?" Her nametag said, Dr. Pine, Emergency Room Physician.

"Yes," Rick replied, moving to her side. "These are his friends."

"Family?"

"Just us. His parents died several years ago, and he didn't have any siblings."

"I see." She stepped closer to the guys as Aiden and Alex came to their feet. "The prognosis is good, but he has to have surgery."

Noah's faced paled as Tori grabbed his hand. "Surgery for what?"

"His spleen is bleeding and he has a laceration on his liver we need to see about."

"English, Doc," Alex said.

"Laceration means he has a wound on his liver. Usually, they heal on their own, but we need to go into his abdomen and see what's going on. He still is not conscious at this time. This doesn't really have me worried based on his blood alcohol level. He was pretty drunk."

Alex moved to his left, the rage he felt almost overwhelming. Dylan could have killed himself or someone else with his stupidity. *He'll be lucky if I don't kill him myself.* "Will he make it?"

"With a little luck, yes, but things can change on a dime. He'll be here for probably a week at least." She pushed her hands into the pockets of her lab coat. "He's lucky. It couldn't have been much worse."

"Can we see him?" Tori asked, her voice small and scared. Noah slipped his arm around her shoulders, bringing her in close to his side.

"I would rather you don't until he is out of surgery. They'll be taking him in shortly. You are more than welcome to wait here." She glanced at the crowd outside the glass. "Or I can show you somewhere more private to wait if you'd like."

Rick held out his hand for her to shake. "We would appreciate that, Doctor. As it is, this will be all over the papers within a few hours."

"Follow me," she said, leading them through a set of double doors that would lock out the world for the time being.

The sterile, white room she led them to left something to be desired. The only color was the aqua blue cushions on the most uncomfortable looking chairs Alex could ever imagine. He hoped they weren't here long.

A coffee machine gurgled in the corner, so he decided to grab a cup if for nothing more than something to do with his hands. Two sugars and three creamers would make the black brew tolerable, he hoped.

Hospitals. He hated hospitals. They were usually the place people went to when there were major issues or to die. If Dylan died, he wouldn't know what to do.

His heart squeezed with worry. It was going to be one hell of a long night.

Aiden paced in front of the doors, his hands balled into fists, and his eyes held something akin to terror. Noah held Tori close on a couch set in the corner, her head on his shoulder as she dabbed at her eyes. Rick fielded phone calls from the press, booking agents, and vendors as he tried to reassure them everything would continue on schedule. How that would happen, Alex wasn't sure. They had a show to do in less than two weeks.

Shoving his hand in his right front pocket, he took a sip of the coffee in the cup and grimaced. The stuff was awful. What he wouldn't give for a big glass of whiskey. The smooth burn would soothe his tangled nerves. He tossed the coffee into the trash.

Madison. He wondered how she was. He'd left in such a hurry, he realized he should call her and explain. Running out right after making love with her wasn't a good way to start anything if that's what he wanted. Their coming together had been so perfect, he didn't want it to end. Touching her, being inside her, seeing the way her eyes closed slowly when she took in everything about the way they'd fit, it was all perfect, more perfect than anything he'd ever experienced before.

"You okay?" Tori touched his arm.

"Yeah, just thinking," he replied, looking down into her face. Tori had become such an important part of the band since she and Noah hooked up, he couldn't think of them without her nearby.

"How is Maddie? She sounded very sick on the phone."

"Much better." He smiled, rubbing his finger over his lips. "I took care of her a bit. Got her some soup, ginger ale, and cold medicine."

Tori wrapped her arms around his waist, hugging him tightly before letting him go. "Thank you. She needed someone to help her. Stubborn is her middle name, I think." She glanced up, catching his gaze. "You really like her, don't you." It wasn't a question. It was something she already knew the answer to, he was afraid.

He shrugged his shoulders, glancing down at the tips of his boots. "Yeah, I guess I do. She's different than the women I usually go out with. She's smart, funny, a little crazy, and a whole lot sexy."

A squeal about broke his eardrum as Tori launched herself into his embrace. "You two are perfect together. I swear."

His heart skittered to a halt. *Perfect together? Oh shit.* "Wait a minute, Tori. I didn't say there was anything permanent going on here. We're having a good time. You know, nothing serious. I can't do serious with all the shit we deal with. Maddie is a nice girl, but she's just another girl in my book. We had a good time. Now, it's time to move on."

A startled gasp brought his gaze up to meet those of the one woman he couldn't stop thinking about, the one he'd made love to not two hours ago.

Maddie stood in the doorway, her hair sticking up as if she haphazardly did something to it so no one would know she'd been thoroughly fucked. Her eyes were wide, uncertainty swimming in the depths, the same ones he'd lost himself in when he'd slid inside her.

"Alex?" she whispered, pain clear in her voice.

What the hell have I done?

Chapter Ten

Torn on whether to go after Maddie or stay where he was, he chose to keep his feet planted. It was better this way. He didn't need a girlfriend anyway. Life on the road was hell. He didn't need to drag a woman into it.

"You are an asshole, Alex." Tori stomped off, back to Noah's side, who now gave him an evil glare.

"What?"

"Did you have to hurt her like that? I mean really, man. She's a nice girl."

"You are in love, dude. You think everyone should be. Let it go. I'm not the settling down kind. You all know that." He walked toward the window to stare out into the late morning sun. It was better this way, better for her and for him. He could go back to his life of a new woman every show, his solitary life on the road, and whatever else he wanted to do.

She'd find someone stable and dependable who would love her ten cats, help pay for that fancy apartment, and have two point five kids. A white picket fence and a big house was in her future, not a rock musician who couldn't even write music these days.

"I'll be back. I need some air." He rushed out through the big double doors, down the hall and out the back entrance to avoid the reporters. Like a bloodhound on a scent, they were relentless when it came to this kind of shit.

For what seemed like miles, he walked, his thoughts in turmoil. Things were in a major upheaval. Not sure what would happen with Dylan, he was scared. Their whole lives might be coming to a screeching halt if their band member died or was even out for a long time. Fans wouldn't understand if they had to cancel several shows, not with the new album. They expected a lot from their favorite band.

Financially, he was set for the rest of his life, if he did well with his investments, but money meant nothing if Dylan died.

He'd known Dylan since high school, even dated his sister for a little while. He wished he knew what was going on with his friend. His current behavior wasn't like him at all. Things had changed a short time ago, but Alex couldn't tie it to anything specific. Friends were forever though. Nothing would change that. Dylan was in for a long fight between healing and legal issues with his stunt.

Alex's thoughts turned to Madison.

He really hadn't meant to hurt her, although he'd been pretty clear about any relationship between them from the get-go. Serious wasn't his thing. The constant touring, the days and nights away, the women throwing themselves at everyone in the band, all of that played hell with anything on a permanent level. He didn't think being with one woman worked for a musician. He'd seen too many give up everything they had for one woman, only to be screwed in the end.

The next block looked familiar. Central Park to his left, his building to his right, and Maddie's across the street.

Standing along the wall that ran along the edge of the park, he stared at her windows, dark and lonely. He didn't know if she'd went home when she left the hospital. Not knowing that much about her, he wasn't sure if she might go to a friend's, out to get drunk, be sitting on her sofa crying her eyes out, or even totally done with him and moved on. He wouldn't blame her if she did.

Horse-drawn carriages clomped past, the staccato rhythm of their hooves echoing in his head like a song, something raw and untamed.

Blown away by the notes bursting in his brain all at once, he raced to the entrance of his building, up the elevator, and into his apartment.

A quick call to Noah to tell him where he was and to call when Dylan was out of surgery, he grabbed his guitar, his pencil, and his songwriting papers, jotting down the notes as fast as he could before he lost them.

Forty-five minutes later, he set the pencil down staring at the paper. It was good. One of the best songs he'd ever written. The pain coming through the notes told him a story. He even had the lyrics, and he didn't do words, he did melody. He couldn't wait to play it for the guys.

His phone rang a moment later.

"Is he out?"

"Yes. You need to come back so we can talk about where we go from here."

"Is he okay?"

"He will be, but it's going to be a long recovery physically, emotionally, and legally."

"I'll be right there." Putting his guitar down, he folded the paper and tucked it into his back pocket before heading down to find a cab since he'd left his car at the hospital.

As he walked outside, he looked up at Madison's building again. He wanted to talk to her, to explain if he could. *Explain what?* The words he'd said to Tori were cruel. Had he really meant them? Right now, he wasn't sure. Everything was in turmoil, and he needed to be there for his friend.

When he arrived at the hospital, he quickly made his way to the waiting room where he'd left his friends a couple of hours before. That had been selfish of him, but he needed the time alone. "Hey," he said, coming through the door.

Noah, Taylor, and Aiden looked up and then away. Apparently, he'd pissed them off. It wouldn't be the first time, nor the last. Tori climbed to her feet, stopping at his side.

The accusatory look she gave him said it all for everyone in the room. "Where have you been?" She wasn't pulling any punches. "You should have been here, Alex. Noah and Aiden needed you. Dylan needed you. You walked out on everyone. I thought these guys were your friends."

"They are."

"You sure don't act like it. What you did was selfish."

He pulled Tori into a hug. "I know and I'm sorry."

"Don't tell me, tell them," she whispered as she put her head on his shoulder for a second. "They are worried sick about Dylan. They didn't need to be worried about you too."

The doctor came out a few minutes later, a younger man maybe about thirty-five. "I'm Dr. Witt. I was the surgeon on your friend's case."

"How is he, Doc?" Noah asked, worry lining his face, making him look much older than his years.

"He will survive, although he has a bit of a recovery ahead. We had to repair his spleen and liver. He's getting some blood right now. You should be able to visit him in a few hours if he's awake and alert. He might be a bit groggy after the surgery."

Noah held out his hand. "Thanks. We appreciate everything you've done for Dylan."

"You're welcome. He's lucky." He shoved his hands into his pockets. "A nurse will come and get you when you can see him."

"We know. We hope he knows as well," Alex said, holding out his hand. "Thank you."

The doctor shook his hand and nodded before he disappeared through the doors, his head held high and his feet in a rush to get to the next patient.

Alex took the moment to reflect on his friends and the worry on their faces. They'd been together so long, he kind of took them for granted. Best friends since high school, they had been through girlfriends, parents, drugs, alcohol, touring, popularity, and hell. It all went together. "Listen, guys. I'm sorry I took off. With everything coming down on me, Madison, Dylan, the tour coming up, and everything else, I just needed some time." He pulled the paper out of his back pocket and handed it to Noah.

"What's this?"

"A song."

Noah's gaze roamed over it several times, taking it all in. "You wrote this when?"

"An hour ago."

"You wrote the whole song in an hour?" Aiden asked, taking the paper from Noah.

"Holy shit, man." Noah took the paper back. "You wrote lyrics? You never do that."

"I know." Alex scuffed his boot on the floor, not meeting their gazes for a moment. "What do you think?"

"I think it's fantastic, Alex. It's raw. The fans will love it."

Tori took the paper from Noah, skimming it for a moment. "Oh my God, Alex. This is perfect. I can't believe you wrote this that fast."

"Sometimes it works that way. I don't know what triggered it, maybe it was all the crap going on, but it came out so fast, I couldn't write it down quick enough."

"The minute Dylan is well enough, we'll bang it out and see how it sounds with all of us." Noah stood up and moved to his side. "This is really good."

"Thanks."

"Next time, don't bail on us. We're a team. We stick together." Noah grabbed him in a hug, pounding him soundly on the back for a second. "Otherwise, I'll kick your ass."

"You wish, man."

"You know I can."

"In your dreams." This was the way things were supposed to be. Joking around, giving each other shit, being there for each other, and having each other's back.

Iron Rogue. His brothers. Their band.

The moment they were able to visit Dylan, they all piled into his room, surrounding his bed as Tori gently touched his hand.

"Dylan?"

Their friend opened his eyes, squinting a second to focus on their faces. "What happened? Where am I?"

"In the hospital, you fucktard," Alex said, moving into Dylan's line of vision. "You hit a fucking tree, man."

"I did what?"

Noah moved closer. "You apparently got drunk, stole a car, and hit a tree. You had surgery a little while ago for a problem with your spleen and liver. You'll have a bit of recovery time ahead of you." The frown on Noah's face said it all. "What the hell were you thinking?"

Dylan's faced paled. "Did I hurt anyone?"

"No, only yourself." Aiden shifted on his feet, nervous to be in the hospital in the first place.

"Thank God."

"Again, dude. What the hell is going on with you that you put yourself in danger like that?"

Dylan's gaze shifted to the doorway. Taylor stood there, apprehension clear on her face. "Taylor."

"Dylan."

Tension was palpable in the room, thick enough you could cut it with a knife. Alex's gaze shifted back and forth between the two of them, realization dawning on him as he watched the exchange.

His friend couldn't keep his secret anymore.

Dylan was attracted to their new keyboardist, and he was fighting it with everything he had.

Rick burst through the door a few minutes later, rushing inside like a tidal wave on the coastline. "You're looking better, Dylan."

"Thanks."

Clearing his throat, Rick commanded the room. "The tour. I've done the best I can to postpone the first several shows. You all know you were supposed to do the first one in Los Angeles in two weeks. The venue wasn't happy. When are they ever? But they've notified all the ticket holders of the rescheduled show. The band is going to have to take a cut in the amount of money they were paying you to make up for lost ticket sales. I don't think there will be many, although the promoter is adamant about the penalty."

Noah grumbled. Alex cussed. Aiden shook his head. Taylor looked lost with what was going on.

"How many more will be doing the same thing?" Alex ran his fingers through his hair, frustration riding him like a dog with a bone.

Rick closed the binder he was reading from. "I'm not sure. I'm still working on the others."

"How many are we going to have to reschedule?" Dylan asked from the bed.

Noah's gaze shifted to him. "The doctor says you'll be out for several weeks. You won't be able to play drums for probably six, so four weeks into our tour."

"How many shows is that?" Aiden had kept quiet until now. He usually didn't ruffle feathers within the group, but he seemed as pissed as the rest of them.

"Ten total."

"Shit." Dylan's face flushed with anger. "I'm sorry, guys."

Always the leader of the group, Noah said what they were all thinking. "We'll make it work. The most important thing is, you're okay."

Tori took Dylan's hand. "You mean the world to everyone here, Dylan. We are here for you, no matter what."

The nurse came in a shooed them all out, saying it was time for his medication, and he needed to rest. Dylan said goodbye to everyone but asked Taylor to stay for a minute. He wanted to talk to her.

Surprised, the rest of the band filed out, even though Alex shot a glance back at the bed for a second before closing the door.

"What's going on?" Aiden said quietly. "I didn't know there was anything between them."

"None of us did," Alex replied. "But I think there is whether it be something uncomfortable or whatever."

The sun had begun to set, casting shadows along the walls of the hospital. Alex realized he hadn't eaten all day and the rest of them probably hadn't either. "How about some food? I don't know about you guys, but I'm starving."

They all mumbled in agreement as they stood outside the door waiting for Taylor to reemerge.

"Should I invite Maddie?" Tori asked, her eyes sparkling with mischief.

He shook his head with a firm stance. "No. I need to talk to her before things become uncomfortable. I know she's your friend, Tori." Tori had her hands on her hips. No messing with that girl when she was upset.

"Yes, she is, and I'm really mad at you for hurting her, Alex. What you said earlier wasn't fair and it wasn't right. You need to apologize."

Not feeling as confident with himself about what he'd said, he murmured, "What I said is the truth."

"I don't think it is. I can see the way you look at her, especially when you don't think anyone is watching. You want her."

Alex ran his fingers through his hair. What was between him and Madison wasn't something he wanted to examine right now. Sure he didn't want anything beyond a casual relationship, he'd pushed her away with his words. Now, if he had to decide what he wanted in this one moment in time, he'd say he wasn't sure anymore. "I don't deny that. Things are complicated with musicians, you know that."

Tori placed her hand on his arm, squeezing in comfort. "They are. I know more than anyone how it works. It depends on how much effort you want to put into it. If she doesn't mean enough to you to make it work, then let her go. She doesn't deserve to be hurt anymore."

Taylor came through the door, breaking the intensity of the conversation. Her eyes held the look of determination and something more. "I'm outta here."

"We're going for food. Would you like to come?" Tori asked, stopping Taylor in her tracks as she looked back over her shoulder.

"Sorry, but no. In fact, I'm not even sure I can continue to play with you guys."

Red infused Noah's face. "What the hell did he say to you?"

Her hand behind her neck, Taylor said, "It doesn't matter, Noah. This is between me and Dylan." Her gaze came up and fixed on Tori. "I don't know how you do it, Tori."

"Do what?"

"Deal with a relationship with a rock star." She twisted away, disappearing out the door without any more explanation.

Alex felt like he'd been kicked in the gut. Realization hit him like a ton of bricks over the head. This was the reason why he wouldn't take things further with Madison. The disappointment he knew she would feel in the long run would kill him.

He'd seen that look in his dad's eyes. Never again.

* * * *

The rollerball under her finger zipped the arrow down the page as she quickly scanned the article stopping on the picture of Alex. It was taken outside of the hospital sometime over the last twenty-four hours. He looked drawn and tired, they all did, the whole group in the picture. The only one not there was Dylan. Not knowing what had happened, only that one of the guys had been hurt, she'd rushed to the hospital to find out. When she'd walked into the room and heard Alex's words, her heart had plummeted into her stomach. He didn't care. Everything they'd shared meant nothing to him. The one thing she'd been afraid of when she'd given in to the attraction between them had come to fruition. She was nothing more than another notch on his belt, another name in his little black book.

Fuck him.

No, that's not right. She couldn't act like she didn't care or that he hadn't hurt her. In the short amount of time they'd spent together over the last couple of weeks, he'd come to mean more to her than he should have.

The way they'd made love, the way he'd taken care of her when she was sick, the way it felt to have him inside her—all of that meant something to her even though it didn't to him.

She leaned back in her chair, her head resting on the rear as she stared at his picture. Was it so wrong to want to comfort him, be there for him, and hold him as the band struggled through this crisis?

Not knowing the extent of Dylan's injuries and what it meant to the band's coming tour schedule, she hesitated to even get involved. She could call Tori, she knew, and find out, but that would be taking advantage of her friendship. It would be wrong on so many levels.

Night gave way to the morning, streaks of sunshine turning the sky to purple as it began to peek over the horizon. A new day dawned. Today, she would have to come to terms with Alex turning his back on her and move on with her life.

She turned in her chair to face the window where she could see Alex's apartment. No light shown through any of the curtains.

Her cell phone sat next to her on the computer desk, mocking her with its silence.

Like a beacon in the night drawing the sailors to the shore, it lit up the darkness in the room as it rang.

The name on the screen. Alex.

It rang three times before she got the nerve to answer.

His voice came across low and sexy. "Hey, babe."

Shivers raced down her arms. "Alex. What's wrong? Is Dylan okay?"

"He will be if I don't kill him first."

"I'm glad he'll be fine. I wouldn't want him to be hurt permanently or anything."

"He'll be out for a few weeks. We won't be able to start our tour for about four to six weeks. The fans are going to be disappointed."

She rubbed her arms, trying desperately to calm her racing heart. "Yeah, but I'm sure they'll understand."

"I hope so. I hate disappointing anyone."

That hurt. He obviously didn't care about doing that to her with the words he'd said at the hospital.

Silence stretched like an echo in a huge room with no barriers to break the sound.

"I miss you," Alex whispered. "I woke up this morning wanting you so badly, I hurt. Holding you the other day was like being on a rollercoaster ride, not knowing where the next turn will be."

"Don't do this, please."

"Maddie. I need to hold you, bury myself inside you, and forget the nightmare of this day."

Should she resist him or give into what was between them even if it was only temporary? Could she handle being the woman of the week for someone like Alex?

Her feet carried her to the door of her apartment before she even could fathom what she was about to do.

With her keys in hand, she jerked open the door.
Alex stood on the other side.

Chapter Eleven

Phones clanked to the floor followed by her keys as their mouths crashed together and he pushed her back inside the apartment before shoving the door closed with his foot. With a quick spin, he had her pinned against the front door. His hands moved over her body, taking her t-shirt up and over her head to bare her breasts to his gaze.

"God, you're beautiful."

His lips danced over her cheek before moving to her jawline where he nipped the skin with his teeth.

Her moans were lost in a breathy sigh the second he sucked the tender skin below her ear into his mouth.

Trapped against the hard panel behind her, she could do nothing but take what he wanted to give her, enjoying each touch, each caress, and each solid plain of his body where it brushed hers.

"Alex," she breathed.

"Maddie." Her name whispered over the wet skin of her neck sent goosebumps racing down her back. "I need you. God, I want you so bad."

One hand held hers above her head while the other mapped the curve of her breast, stopping to brush his callused fingertips over the nipple. The roughness sent a bolt of electricity straight to her pussy. The low moan escaping her lips sounded needy and desperate, nothing like what she wanted to be with Alex until the moment he stood on the other side of the door.

His mouth came back to hers, devouring her with his lips, his tongue, and his teeth. His hand left her breast only to skim down her side, before reaching around to the waistband of the boy shorts she'd worn tonight while she worked.

The second his fingers dipped between her pussy lips, she went up on her toes, a throaty sound escaping with a sigh.

"So fucking wet for me."

"Please."

His lips closed over the tip of her breast, sucking the nipple deep into his mouth as his fingers pressed inside her. Her legs shook, unable to hold her any longer. A choking sob left her lips as a mind-numbing orgasm washed over her out of nowhere.

Forehead pressed to hers, his gaze locked on her face the second she opened her eyes.

"Maddie?" He released her hands, allowing her to lower her arms.

Realization washed over her. He'd done it again, used her to satisfy his need to be close to someone without regard to her feelings at all. "I think you should go."

He closed his eyes for a second before stepping back with a sharp nod. "I'm sorry. I didn't come over here—"

It didn't matter that I was about to go over to his apartment and beg him to make love to me. "Just go."

Grabbing his phone from the floor, he opened the door, glanced at her one last time and then disappeared down the hall. She slowly shut it behind him, wishing he'd never called, wishing she'd never met him, and wishing he'd leave her alone. Somehow, she didn't think that was the answer she sought, but it would protect her heart. Probably not.

Tears streaked down her cheek as she slid to the floor, rocking herself with her arms around her waist. She didn't want to feel this way. She didn't want to need him so badly. God help her, she didn't want to love him, but she did.

After several minutes, the tears stopped, she pulled herself up, and headed into the bathroom. A long, hot bath would feel really good right now, and then maybe she could think about what to do from here. Her life wasn't over because she'd turned her back on Alex Rockly.

Hot water enveloped her as she sank into the tub, the scent of lavender surrounding her from the essential oils she'd put in while she'd run the bath. Her back rested on the rear of the tub, eyes closed, attempting to relax and forget about the last hour.

Not an easy thing to do.

Alex's face swam in front of her closed eyelids. The tension in his body came off him in waves of anguish she wanted to soothe. He'd said he needed her. How could she turn away from someone who needed what she could give? It wasn't in her nature to do that. Her parents had always called her a nurturer and she was. She wanted to take care of others, help them in ways only she could, and be there for someone in need. It was the whole reason she volunteered on a monthly basis at the women's shelter. The time spent there made her feel whole. Money could do a lot, but holding a woman while she cried over being severely beaten by someone she thought loved her, was something she could give back.

Love manifested in strange ways sometimes.

Odd how she'd fallen in love with a man who has commitment issues and one who couldn't come to terms with a relationship that lasted more than a few weeks. When she pictured the man she'd settle down with, he'd always been a stable guy, someone who wouldn't stray, and someone who would be home every night for supper and to play with their kids before they went to bed. Then they would curl up together after making love that night, talk about their day, and fall asleep in each other's arms. Never once did she imagine having feelings for a man like Alex.

The tension in her shoulders eased a little. A decision had to be made. Could she walk away from her feelings for him, could she forgive and forget the hurtful words he'd said, and could she make him realize what they had might be something he's always wanted? The tangled web of feelings made it difficult. He wanted her, there was no doubt about that. Did he love her? She had no idea.

You can't make someone love you. It didn't work. If he really didn't care, then she had no choice but to walk away.

The water began to cool, forcing her to get out of the bath. Sunlight reflected off a mirror on the wall, refracting light in several directions. The noises of the city reached her ears from below on the streets. The day had begun. People were headed to work, school, or wherever else they needed to be. Life went on without her input for the day. Sleep would be a blessed relief from the thoughts rushing through her brain.

Crawling beneath the cool, white sheets, she snuggled down into the softness and closed her eyes. Dreams claimed her a short time later, unfortunately, one blond rock star was the center of those imaginings.

* * * *

Alex forced his gritty eyelids open, squinting into the sunlight across his face. *Surely, it can't be morning already? I don't think I slept more than a couple of hours.* His mouth tasted like something had crawled inside and died during the night. Grit met his tongue when he ran it across the surface of his teeth. *Gross. That's what I get for drinking so heavy before I passed out.* The moment he'd returned to his apartment last night, whiskey had been his friend. His visit to Maddie had gone terribly wrong, not the giving her an orgasm part, he loved feeling her come apart on his hand. Using her like that felt all kinds of immoral. His intention when he'd left his apartment headed for hers was to talk. He wanted to convince her that he hadn't meant to hurt her with his words, but the moment she opened the door, his thoughts went haywire. He couldn't think beyond that sexy little t-shirt and shorts she'd had on, her legs long and bare, and those cute little toes with the pink nail polish on them. Yes, he wanted her with every breath he took. Losing himself inside her had been a wish, something he hadn't planned on enacting, but things got out of control the moment their mouths touched. His hands had a mind of their own, it seemed, and she'd been right there with him.

He felt like shit for taking advantage of her. The whiskey blanked his mind last night. This morning, not so much.

His cell phone rang somewhere from his pants pocket on the floor. After rolling off the bed onto his knees, he grabbed the jeans and fished for it. "Hello?"

"What the hell have you done, Alex?"

"Good morning, Tori."

"You are such a bastard. I should kill you right now."

"I probably wouldn't be missed, the way I feel at the moment." He grabbed his head, the pounding between his ears almost drowning out the screeching from his best friend's girl on the other side of the phone. "Easy, Tori."

"Don't you easy me, Mister. You took advantage of Maddie last night and I'm pissed."

He leaned back against the bed, holding the phone out from his ear as she continued to rant for several minutes.

When quiet had descended for a moment, he said, "I already apologized to her, but I plan to make it up to her today."

"What are you going to do?"

"I'm not sure yet. I just woke up with a splitting hangover, so it will take me a minute to get my wits together."

Her voice quieted as she replied, "Alex. I know you care about her. Why are you putting both of you through this?"

Images flashed through his brain. His parents and the disappointment on their faces tore up his gut. He didn't want to put anyone else through that torment. He wouldn't be able to handle that look on Maddie's face. "There are things you don't understand, Tori. Things from my past."

"Nothing is more important than love."

"Love can't fix everything."

"It can if you let it, Alex. Look at Noah. He was a mess before him and I got together, and now he's the happiest he's ever been in his life. We are together for the long haul, no matter what and you can have that, too, if you let her in."

He rested his head against the mattress, his eyes closed, and his stomach twisted into a knot. "A musician's life is shit. The constant touring, the promotions, the women in our faces all the time. You know how the song goes."

"What's that?"

"The road ain't no place to start a family."

"And if I remember the song, it's called Faithfully and the musician lives by his love with the woman no matter how hard it is to be apart."

"I'm not sure I can do that, Tori."

"You can if you love her."

Love her. Did he really love Maddie? He wasn't sure. Love was a difficult emotion for him, one he didn't know if he would recognize if it bit him on the ass. He cared about her that much he knew. "I don't know what love is."

"You love the guys in the band, like brothers, right?"

"Yeah."

"Then you know what love is, Alex. When you care about someone to the point that you can't think about anything but them, what their needs are and put those above your own, then it's love. I would do anything for Noah and he would do the same for me."

"I'm glad for you two."

"Do you want to be in love?"

"I'm not sure." His lips twisted into a wry smile. "I kind of like having a different woman every night."

Tori laughed into the phone. "You're a liar too, Alex Rockly. You haven't been with a woman in months."

"Noah has a big mouth."

"Pillow talk."

"He still has a big mouth."

"A sexy one, yes. Big? Hmm. Not sure on that one."

"I don't need to hear about your sex life, Tori. It makes me horny."

A rolling laugh met his ear through the phone. "Not an image I want, Alex." She was silent for several seconds. "What do you want from your relationship with Maddie?"

"Hell if I know. Sex. Fantastic sex."

"What else?"

"I like waking up next to her." He rubbed his eyes with his hand. "I've never woken up next to anyone before her yesterday. Is that weird or what?"

"For a rock star, nope."

He waited for what seemed like a long time before he answered. "You know, being a rock star isn't all it's cracked up to be."

"I have one more question and then you can figure out what you're going to do. I will warn you though, don't hurt her again. If you really care about her, don't do it. Let her go now."

"What's the question, Tori?"

"Do you want to spend the rest of your life alone?"

He couldn't answer that right at that second, so he let it drop. "Bye, Tori."

"Bye, Alex."

He clicked off his phone, tossing it to the floor several feet away to keep the temptation of calling Maddie to a minimum. The decision he faced wasn't one he could do without some coffee, breakfast, and a shower, not necessarily in that order.

An hour later, he felt better. A nice long shower, a shave, and some coffee put a whole new perspective on what he wanted.

What he wanted was Madison Avery.

His plan? He didn't have one except that he needed to change the way he played this because he didn't want to be the asshole rock star he was known to be since Iron Rogue hit the big times. He'd come to realize the women in his life up to that point were shallow, fortune-seeking whores who slept with anyone who would give them a little attention. Most wanted the flashing lights, camera's, and to be the woman on his arm. If he gave them a few sparkly things, they would be happy to leave him alone. A diamond necklace, a pair of emerald earrings, or a gold bracelet and they would disappear quickly enough.

The realization of how shallow his own life had become hit him like a ton of bricks.

First things first.

He grabbed his cell from the floor where he'd tossed it and dialed his mother's number.

"Hello?"

"Hey, Mom. It's Alex."

"Oh my God. Alex?"

"Yeah, it's me. Sorry I haven't called lately. Things have been a bit crazy here."

"Dad, it's Alex! Come here, quick." He heard shuffling and then the phone went to speaker. "It is so good to hear your voice."

"Hey, son. How are things going?"

"Good, I guess. I'm in New York at the moment."

"New York? Wow," his father said. "You have a place there, right?"

"Yeah. An apartment near Central Park."

"How are things with the other boys?" his mother asked.

Alex laughed. They hadn't been boys in a long time. "The guys are fine, Mom. Well other than Dylan. He got into a car accident a day or two ago and was hurt pretty badly."

"Oh my goodness. Tell him I will keep him in my prayers."

Dylan grimaced. His parents were a lot more religious than he was. Yeah, he believed in God, but he didn't do the church thing even though he'd grown up going to church every Sunday. "I will." He needed to breathe. Talking to his parents always made him feel so young and small like he couldn't think for himself. He was a grown man, could make his own decisions without his parents' approval.

"Honey?"

"I'm still here."

"You okay?"

"Yeah. I'm feeling a little homesick. I wanted to let you know I'm coming home this weekend to visit for a few days. We were supposed to start touring soon, but Dylan's accident has forced us to delay a few weeks."

His mother sighed for a moment, making him think he might not be welcome. "Alex, you are welcome anytime, honey. You know that. We love you."

Emotions clogged his throat. He wanted to say those three words, but he held his tongue. "I'll see you this evening then."

"Do you need us to pick you up at the airport?"

"No, I'll bring our plane."

"All right then. We'll see you later tonight."

He hung up the phone, pacing by the end of his bed. He wanted to tell Madison he'd be gone for a few days. He didn't though. She probably didn't care anyway. He dialed Noah, and Tori picked up. "Hey, Tori."

"Hey yourself."

Pushing his fingers through his hair, he stuck the phone between his cheek and shoulder so he could tie the long mess of hair back off his neck. "Tell Noah I'll be heading back to Iowa for a few days. I'm taking the plane in case they want to know where it is."

Silence.

"I need to put some things to rest."

"Okay. You know Dylan will be out of the hospital on Saturday."

"Yeah, but he'll be okay, I'm sure. He can hire a nurse to help him around the house or whatever. Hell, he can stay here if he wants. I won't be here anyway, and he can watch my place while I'm gone."

"Are you all right?"

He pushed a sigh between his lips, wishing he didn't have to explain anything to her. "I'll be okay. I need a few days with my folks to work some things out."

"Are you letting Maddie know you'll be gone?"

"No." He sat down on the side of the bed, wiping his sweaty palms on the thighs of his jeans. "I'm sure she doesn't care anyway and it will be awkward with how things went down last night."

"I get it, Alex. I wish you would talk to her anyway."

"I will, but I need to do this first."

"Leave her a note maybe?"

"Maybe." He grabbed a bag and started shoving clothes in it. A couple of pairs of jeans, three shirts, a sweatshirt because it was beginning to turn colder in Iowa, a pair of boots, his sneakers, a few toiletries, and he'd be set. "I need to go. I have to finish packing and call the pilot so he can get the plane ready."

"Be careful. We love you even if you are a stubborn asshole."

He grinned despite the knot in his gut. "Thanks, Tori."

"See you soon."

He hung up the phone, dialed the pilot, and set about getting the rest of his things together. It was going to be hell for a few days. Home wasn't always the sanctuary one thought it would be when they grew up. His wasn't in his mind anyway. His childhood hadn't been that bad, really, just the typical teenage angst. Parents were parents although their break up had hurt him. They supported his school stuff, the few sports things he'd tried, and then shit had hit the fan when the guitar came out. At first, they didn't care. It had only been a fad he was going through. Playing a little here and there didn't account for much. When he'd found the electric guitar, things had changed. Rock became his life and his love. School sucked, but he'd made it through, by the skin of his teeth, to get his diploma. Talk of college stalled the moment he'd blown up in a screaming match with his dad.

He'd left home that night, not returning for several years. Aiden's mom had given him a place to live while they banged out song after song, killing themselves trying to get a record deal, working at smoky bars for peanuts. Alcohol and drugs got him through. Cocaine had been his drug of choice for a long time. He'd kicked that habit a few years ago after one hard night of partying after a show, and he'd found himself somewhere he didn't recognize with people he didn't know. Scared out of his mind, he got back to the hotel and swore off all drugs. Alcohol he still did occasionally, like last night. The hangover it caused did nothing for him anymore. Cottonmouth and feeling like shit didn't make things better.

He glanced at his phone, debating whether to text or call Maddie. The way they'd parted last night was bad, real bad. Grabbing it in his hand, he opened his contacts and pushed talk.

It rang several times and then went to voicemail.

"Hey, Maddie. Listen, I'm sorry about everything, last night, what I said at the hospital, the whole thing. I shouldn't be saying this in a voicemail. I want to talk to you in person, but I'm going home to Iowa for a few days to work out some things. I'll call you when I get back to New York and hopefully, you'll still see it in your heart to talk to me." He hesitated for a second, wanting to say more, even though he wasn't sure what to say. "Talk care, babe."

After hanging up, he grabbed his bag and headed downstairs, locking the apartment behind him.

This was going to be one of the most difficult things to do that he'd ever faced.

Chapter Twelve

The phone lit up with Alex's name and then went black. Madison didn't answer his call, preferring to let it go to voicemail.

Even after a long bath last night, she still felt dirty and used, like her feelings didn't matter to him one bit. She should have known this would be the way things would work out. He had everything he ever wanted, women, money, and fame. What would he want with a nobody nerdy girl like her anyway? She wasn't anything special to anyone, much less someone like him.

Her life would go on like before. Her work, her cats, and her friends. What more could she want, right?

Tag jumped up in her lap, begging for petting, rubbing against her hand, starved for attention. "You are such a spoiled cat." She pressed a kiss to his head. "I love you."

The little envelope in the corner told her there was a voicemail. For now, it could wait.

She'd slept little during the last several hours. Alex making love to her over and over had haunted her dreams. Horny as hell when she woke up, she had to force herself to orgasm with your dildo to get a little relief, and even then it didn't help all that much.

Work required her attention. She had a deadline on a program she had to finish and even if she worked round the clock for the next several days, she might not get it done in time.

Coffee at her elbow, she pulled up her computer, she logged into her program and got to work. Keeping her mind on the task at hand would help her get over this fascination with Alex.

Yeah, it sounded good.

The sun began to fade behind the buildings, making Maddie realize she'd spent several hours on the computer without thinking about Alex more than twenty-five times an hour. She'd managed to get some of her work done without stopping to flip through news articles with his picture, usually with some leggy blonde on his arm. Damn him anyway.

Wine. That's what I need. A big glass of wine.

White. Red. It didn't matter. Wine was wine and it would make her mind go numb at least for a little bit. Maybe she'd even be able to sleep tonight or today, whichever it was when she finished working.

Glass in hand, she glanced out the sliding glass doors toward Alex's apartment. It was dark. No lights on anywhere.

Her cell phone jingled in the office where it sat on the desk. The ringtone told her it was Tori, but she wasn't sure she wanted to talk to her friend right then. Her connection to Alex made it hard to talk to her.

I could use a friend right now though.

"Hey, Tori. What's up?"

"How are you?"

Maddie took a seat at her desk, folding her legs up under her to get comfortable. "I'm good. Having a glass of wine at the moment, trying to relax so I can get more work done. I have a huge deadline coming up."

"I'm sorry. I didn't mean to disturb you."

"You didn't. I was taking a break anyway." Maddie took a sip of her wine, setting it down on the corner of her desk. "How is Dylan? I haven't heard anything, but I hope he's doing better."

"He is. He'll be out of the hospital on Saturday."

"Good. Did he give you guys any indication of what the hell he was thinking?"

"Nope. Not a clue. None of us know anything about what happened or why he stole a car and wrecked it. At least not yet. Something weird is going on between him and Taylor though."

"Oh?"

"Yeah."

"Hmm." She paused, hoping Tori would give her a clue as to why she'd called. "How's Noah?"

"He's good. Trying to get things together so when they go on tour in a few weeks, everything will be set."

"That's great. He's such an organizer. No wonder he's the leader of the band." Silence filled the line for several seconds.

"Maddie?"

"Yeah?"

"Have you heard from Alex?"

There it was. The reason for the call. "He called earlier, but I didn't answer. I think he left a voicemail. I haven't looked yet though."

"You might want to."

"Why?" Terror filled her chest. "Is something wrong? Is he okay?"

"Not sure. He's not hurt or anything, I don't think." Tori sighed. "I don't want to say anything. Just listen to the voicemail, okay?"

"I will. As soon as I hang up with you." Terrified something bad had happened, she hung up with Tori a short time later and dialed her voicemail.

His voice filled her head as she listened, relieving a bit of the squeeze around her heart. He talked about I'm sorry's, how he needed to fix something in Iowa, and how he hadn't meant for things to get out of control last night. She couldn't blame him for that one. She wanted it as badly as he did, but when everything was said and done, she'd felt emotionally unstable and stepping back became a survival instinct.

She glanced at the clock. He would be in Iowa, more than likely. Not necessarily out of reach by phone, although out of reach physically. The hurt in his voice, the need for an emotional connection—all of that tore her apart wanting to be there for him even if she'd thought about letting him go and moving on. Good Lord, she was a mess.

For now, he needed to come to her and make things right. It would be hard, she knew. Waiting him out might be the death of her. She had to though, for her own sanity and heart.

What if he didn't?

She'd deal with it when the time came. She was tired of being the doormat for Alex Rockly and his sexy ass. It was time to pull up her big girl panties and put him in his place. No more being used. He would have to give her something besides a quick fuck here and there. Those were nice and all, but she needed more. If he wasn't willing to give it, then so be it.

Needing a distraction from her thoughts, Maddie turned on the television, flipping through channels trying to find the news. One channel caught her attention, flashing a picture of the band. *So much for a distraction.*

The reporter came on sitting behind a huge desk. Her hair in a wild mess around her head, making her look like she'd been freshly fucked, her red lipstick gave her mouth a huge look, her colored contacts were definitely fake, and her boobs could be nothing but silicon. "Tonight we take a look at the band Iron Rogue and the plague of problems they've had in recent months. First, we go back to a few months ago when lead singer, Noah King forced the band into a hiatus due to some personal issues. His father had fallen ill. The diagnosis—cancer. Our condolences to him and his family in the passing of the patriarch a few weeks ago. He has since hooked up with the former reporter for Rock Band News, Victoria Richmond. We hear they are tight as thieves and enjoying each other's company immensely if you get my drift."

"What a bitch."

"Next is Aiden Rains. Aiden hasn't been up to much, so nothing new to report there. He's the same happy-go-lucky dude he's always been. No new love interests."

"Sorry to disappoint you," Maddie grumbled. The woman had no couth at all. It was all about the story.

"Dylan Mannix is another story, folks. He got drunk a few days ago, stole a car, and ran it into a tree causing irreparable damage to the car and ended up in the hospital with some major injuries including spleen and liver issues. The band was by his side, including a possible new love interest in the band's brand new keyboardist, Taylor Valentine. More to come on that one."

"She doesn't know a fucking thing. God, what a way to tear the band apart. Sheesh."

"Last but certainly not least is Alex Rockly. Rumor has it there is something stirring in his life. A new love? Problems at home in Iowa? We aren't sure. He's been seen around town with this woman."

Madison's picture flashed on the screen, making her gasp. "Where the hell did they get that?" It was an old picture, one from her interview days with various computer companies when she'd graduated college. It wasn't even a flattering picture.

"Her name. Madison Avery. She is a computer whiz with a major company here in New York, and she is definitely not looking at Alex's money. She has her own from some big computer programs she owns the patent on and bonuses she's received for her work, from what we've been able to dig up."

"Holy hell," she whispered, not sure how to even take the dig into her personal life.

"As for the problems in Iowa, word has it there are issues with his parents. Something big may be coming down the pike, folks. Is Alex leaving the band for his would-be love? What about Dylan and his legal issues as well as monetary issues with this latest fiasco?" The camera zoomed in on the reporters face. "Stay tuned. We will have the most up to date information on Iron Rogue coming soon." The woman blinked her eyes several times before the camera faded to black and a new commercial came on the screen.

Madison exhaled and leaned back in her chair. If this was the kind of crap the guys had to put up with all the time, no wonder they avoided the limelight as much as they could. The constant digging into their personal lives had to suck. Betrayal was a hard pill to swallow when all of your personal information was now out there for everyone who wanted to know. The tie to Alex put her out there now. If she wanted something permanent with him, that would become her life. Every time she went to the grocery store without makeup on, it would be on the front page of every rock magazine in the country. Was Tori even aware of the kind of transparency her life would be?

Grabbing her cell off the desk, she dialed Tori's number.

"Hey, girlfriend. What's up?"

"Did you see the broadcast on the band that was just on television?"

"Nope. Why?"

"You might want to. It's bad. They have all kinds of crap on there from Dylan being in the hospital to me being seen with Alex, what I do for a living, how much money I have, and everything."

"Maddie, listen to me." She could hear a door closing in the background. "If you let this get to you, it will drive you nuts. As a reporter myself, I know how these people work. They'll dig and dig until they find something, anything to sell a story."

"Did you used to be that way?"

"Yeah, unfortunately, I did. That's kind of how I ended up with Noah, but that's another piece to our puzzle." Maddie heard a creak of something. "The guys know this. They've been in this business for quite a while and they do their best to keep on the down low, but things come out, pictures are taken without their knowledge, and they have to deal with it. The more negative the reporters can spin the story, the better. This is why they have a PR person who is on top of it always. It will be okay, I promise."

"But Tori, they have a picture of me! They've splashed all my information on this program, where I work and everything. Privacy will be a thing of the past." The buzzer on her intercom went off. "Hang on. Someone is at the door."

She walked into the living room and toward the front entrance. Her security camera by the buzzer was lit up and a face stood right in front of the camera.

"Can I help you?"

"Are you Madison Avery?"

"Yes. Why?"

"I am Ringo Madrid with Rock Band News. I want to talk to you about Alex Rockly."

Tori's voice reached her through the phone. "Do not let him in, Maddie. He's a shark who works for the magazine I used to be at. He'll tear you up."

"I'm sorry, but no comment," she said, shutting off the intercom before pushing another button to call the doorman.

"I'm sorry, Ms. Madison. I'm trying to keep them at bay, but there are dozens of people out here wanting to talk to you."

"Call the police then, James. They can't block the entrance and I'm not coming out to talk to them."

"Yes, ma'am."

"Good girl," Tori replied. "You did great!"

"Thanks, but have you thought about how this kind of crap is going to impact your life now that you're with Noah?"

Tori sighed into the phone. "Madison, Noah is my life. I would do anything for him. If it means dealing with some nosy reporters, who by the way I am one of, some women throwing themselves at him, or him being gone a lot, then so be it. I will kick the women's asses into next week. I will handle the nosy reporters with the finesse of a woman in love, and the being gone part will be handled with video chats, phone calls, and going with him as much as I can. I love him. All of this is minor compared to that."

Minor compared to love. That's what I want. Love that means everything.

Her heart sank. Could she have that with Alex? She wasn't so sure anymore.

* * * *

The hard bump as the plane hit the ground jarred Alex from the fitful sleep he'd fallen into after he boarded the plane in New York. Grit behind his eyelids made them itchy and dry. Sleep wasn't all it was cracked up to be apparently.

"We've landed, sir. We'll be on taxi for a minute, though, before we reach our parking spot."

"Thanks," he replied, shouting to be heard through the door to the cockpit where the pilot sat. "Great. Why did I come here again?" He rubbed his tired eyes with his hand before letting it fall to his side. "Oh yeah, clear the air with the parental units." He grimaced before stretching his tired limbs out from the cramped seat since he'd forgotten to lay it out. "This was such a fabulous idea."

The plane rolled to a halt as the engines powered down. Alex grabbed his duffle bag and waited for the pilot to emerge from the cockpit and open the door.

"I hope the flight wasn't too bumpy," he said, his gaze moving over Alex's face.

"No. Not bad. I slept most of it."

The door lowered to the ground and the pilot hurried down the steep stairs. When Alex got a look outside, a black sedan waited with his buddy standing next to it. Ethan pulled him into one of those brotherly hugs with a slap to the back. "Good to see you, Alex."

"I haven't been gone that long, man."

"No, but you look like shit. What the hell have you been doing in New York? Partying until the sun comes up every night?"

"Not really, no, but sleep has been evasive the last few nights." Alex went around to the passenger side and slid in as Ethan started the engine. "Thanks for picking me up."

"No problem. Can't leave my guys hanging at the airport thumbing it to town." The car pulled out through the private gates and out onto the highway. "What's the trip for? I know the rest of the band is back in New York."

"Yeah, this is personal."

"Hmm." Silence enveloped them for several minutes. "Want to talk about it?"

"Not really."

"Women troubles?"

"No. Yeah. Sort of, I guess. I met a girl in New York."

"A girl?" Ethan rubbed his chin before shooting a glance at Alex. "Wow."

Alex wasn't sure he knew what that meant. "Wow, what?"

"I've never heard you refer to a woman you've fucked as a girl. They are band whores, groupies, or just women."

"How do you know I've even fucked her?"

Ethan broke into a hearty laugh, something deep and belly rolling as he drove along trying to keep the car on the road. "You? I don't know a woman alive you haven't fucked if you wanted to."

Alex frowned as he thought about Maddie. She wasn't the type of girl you just fucked, she was special. Yeah, he liked being inside her a lot, but that wasn't all there was. She'd wormed her way into his thoughts on a very regular basis, something he wasn't used to, and she'd remained there. "Okay, so yeah, I've fucked her, but it's not like that."

"Whoa." Ethan cut him a glance. "This is serious shit, man."

Things were strained with Maddie, he knew that. It was something he would deal with when he got back to New York. Right now, he needed to put some of these feelings between him and his parents to bed so he could move on and hopefully become a better person—a person someone like Maddie might really be interested in. "I'm not here because of that. I need to clear the air with my parents."

Ethan held up one hand. "It's okay, Alex. I know you had some rough shit with them over the whole college thing when you were in high school."

"Yeah, I did, and it's time to deal with it."

"Cool, but hey. If you want to go out later and have a beer or something, let me know."

The car pulled up in front of his parents' house. The lights were on, the front door stood open behind the white screen door, and music from the eighties played in the background.

Alex gave Ethan a high five. "Thanks again. I'll call you later."

"Sure. Take it easy."

The door shut behind him as he stepped up on the curb with his duffle in hand. He took a long breath in and blew it out to steady his nerves before approaching the front door. Unsure whether to knock or just walk in, he hesitated for a moment too long.

"Alex, you can come in, son," his father said through the screen door as he pushed it open. "You are always welcome here."

"Thanks, Dad."

His father had the same coloring as he himself did. Blond hair and blue eyes were prominent on the male side of the Rockly's. His mother, on the other hand, was dark haired and dark eyed as were Alex's two sisters. Alex noticed how his father seemed to have aged since he'd seen him last. Lines near his eyes and mouth seemed deeper. His face looked a bit drawn like he'd not slept well lately.

His father put his hand on Alex's back, leading him into the living room where he put his duffle on the ottoman near the couch.

"Where's Mom?"

"In the kitchen making you something to eat. We figured you hadn't had supper since you left New York."

Alex's mother knew him well. He was always up for food. "Mom?"

"I'll be out in a minute, Alex. Do you want something to drink with your sandwich?"

"Milk is fine."

"Coming right up."

Alex took a seat on the couch, his stomach heavy as if a boulder sat in the bottom. Clammy palms reminded him that this wasn't going to be easy. He'd never brought up the topic in all the years since he'd left even though he'd been home a few times. It was time to clear the air.

His mother arrived, plate and glass in hand, giving it to him before taking a seat further down the couch from where he sat. A bite into the bread revealed his favorite, roast beef and cheddar. "Thanks. You always made the best sandwiches, Mom."

Furtive glances between his parents made him realize they were nervous about this conversation too.

The minute he finished his food and set the plate aside, he turned back toward his parents. "Mom. Dad. We need to talk."

His father scooted forward on the chair where he'd taken a seat, his gaze fixed on Alex's as if trying to read his face. His mother gripped his father's hand, her knuckles white with tension. Searching his face for an answer, she turned to his father and then back to him.

"Alex, honey. We love you no matter what, remember that."

"I know, Mom, but this is something I need to get out there in the open because it's been bothering me for a long time."

"Son. You're gay, right?"

Chapter Thirteen

Alex burst out laughing, his gut hurting so badly, that he almost fell to the floor in hysterics. The look on his parent's faces made him laugh that much harder. After several minutes, he wiped his eyes and faced them. "God no."

His father breathed a heavy sigh of relief while his mother squeezed his hand.

"I'm glad you would accept that part of me if I was, but no. I am attracted to women and have always been that way. I have no desire to sleep with a man."

"Oh, thank goodness." The sigh of relief coming from his mother almost made him laugh again. "Not that we wouldn't love you anyway, Alex, but we know how young people are these days and how more and more are realizing they love someone of the same sex."

He needed that laugh to ease the tension in his gut. This discussion wasn't going to be easy regardless. With his head down and his hands dangling between his parted knees, he said, "I want to talk to you about the issue with me not going to college."

"Really, Alex? That was so long ago," his father replied.

Raising his head, he met his father's gaze. "It's bothering me and has been for some time. I need to clear the air."

"All right."

His vision clouded for a moment as his thoughts raced back to that terrible day. His parents had been bugging him for a while about applying to colleges in the area and following in his father's footsteps. He'd been avoiding it at all cost. His heart lie in the guitar, and he and the guys had started practicing hardcore, working out songs so they could get one recorded.

The band had spent the afternoon in Aiden's mother's garage pounding out a song they thought might be the one. The melody flew from his fingers in a long string of notes, perfectly blended to make a great song. Noah had already come up with the lyrics and it was on Alex to bring everything together. He'd done it. The song?

Dare to Love.

When he'd come home, he'd been excited, hyped up on adrenaline after they'd put everything together that afternoon and made an appointment with a recording studio several miles away to get it on tape. The moment he'd walked through the door, his life had imploded.

Alex shook his head, bringing his thoughts back to the present, in the living room of his family home. "After you two divorced, it was hard on me. I had to become the man of the house. You were around, but not nearly as much as when you lived here."

"I'm sorry for that. I needed to try harder to be the father I should have been." His dad grasped his mother's hand. "Things worked out in the long run even though I know how rough it was on you all."

"I'm sure you remember the afternoon I came home from practicing with the band and we argued. I don't actually remember why you were here that afternoon with mom, but it changed my life.

"Of course. I felt terrible after you left, Alex."

"You did?"

"Yes." His father wiped his hand on the thigh of his pants. "I realized then I was pushing you to be me and it wasn't what you wanted at all. I wanted you to follow me into architecture, but you never had the drive to do that kind of work." He sighed. "You doodled, yes, but you didn't draw with a passion, wanting to make things that would wow the world once it was built." A chuckle escaped his lips. "Little did I know it would be your sister who would find her way in the world of building."

Suzy was three years younger than Alex and had become an architect like their father. From the time he could remember, she'd sit for hours and draw and color until she had whatever it was just right.

"Music was my passion, Pop."

"I know that, son. I should have opened my eyes and realized that long before you left that day. I was terrified things wouldn't work out for you and failure would be imminent." A soft chuckle left his father's lips. "I should have known you'd do well. You were always so driven to succeed. There wouldn't have been any other ending to what you wanted to do." His father's gaze fixed on his face. "We are very proud of you, Alex, even if you don't think so. We've even been to a few of your shows, the last one being a few months ago."

"You were? Why didn't you tell me? I would have got you front row and backstage."

"You were working, son. You don't disturb a man when he's working," his mother added. She shook her head and patted his knee. "I'm worried about you though, with all those women. You need to find a nice girl, someone stable, pretty, and that won't take your shit."

"Mom!"

"I'm serious. You need to settle down."

He thought of Madison. His parents would like her. She was the type his mother would think perfect for him. "There is a girl."

His mother's face lit up like someone stuck her finger in a socket. "There is? What's her name? Where does she live? What's she like?"

Another chuckle left his lips. "Easy, Mom." His thoughts sobered a bit. "I'll get to that, but we need to hammer out this other stuff first." He ran his fingers through his hair. "I need to say I'm sorry for blowing up that day. I knew you only wanted what was best for me, and I took it very personally that you couldn't understand music was what I wanted with my whole heart." A heavy sigh escaped his mouth. "You see, that day our hit song for the band came together. All the music, all the lyrics—everything. It was perfect. We even made an appointment to record it in a studio so we could send it to the record companies." His gaze met his father's. "I'm proud of that song to this day. It made Iron Rogue. It put us on the map, and I wrote those notes."

"We know."

He jumped to his feet, agitated they still weren't listening. "No, you don't! I wanted to share that excitement with you, but all you could do was hand me the letter of acceptance to a college I hadn't chosen, for a program I didn't want!"

His father wearily climbed to a standing position. "Alex, please listen to me." His father held out his hand toward the couch, giving Alex the option of sitting back down or walking out again.

His chose to sit.

"I was wrong for doing that application for you, I know that. I thought I knew what was best for you. I didn't listen to you at all when you tried to tell me about your music and how much you enjoyed the guitar." Daniel took a few steps to stand behind Alex's mother, placing his hands on her shoulders. "I'm sorry. You mean the world to me. I just wanted what was best for my son."

Alex let his gaze focus out the window to his left for a moment. He'd known all of this, figured it out some time ago, but stubborn was his middle name or should have been. The animosity was killing his relationship with them, and he didn't want that anymore. It felt wrong on so many levels. He knew in his heart, it was time. The bitterness had to end. "I'm sorry too. I was so angry that day, I wasn't thinking straight. All I could see was red when you handed me that acceptance letter. You were making the decision for me, right then, and I hated you for it."

"I know you did. There has been this wedge between us for a long time. I hope now we can move forward."

Alex moved next to his mother, putting his arm around her back. "I love you both. I hope now you understand my love for music and that the band is the right thing for me."

Andrea put her hand on his cheek. "We've never doubted you would do well at whatever you chose to do." A tear slipped down her cheek. "We were scared for our baby boy, that's all."

"Thanks, Mom. Thanks, Dad."

She patted his hand. "Now. Tell me about this girl!"

Alex laughed for a second, taking her hand in his. "Her name is Madison Avery and she lives in New York. You'd love her, Mom. She's smart, funny, a great friend, and has ten cats."

"Holy cow! Ten?"

He shook his head, amazed at how Madison made it look easy with all of those felines. "Yes, ten. She has an apartment in the building next to mine. She's a computer wiz and writes programs for them. The way she can make a computer do what she wants it to do amazes me. I'm lost with those things."

"She sounds amazing." Andrea clapped her hands together like a small child. Alex grinned. "When do we get to meet her?"

He could feel his mouth twist in a grimace. "I'm not sure. She's kind of mad at me right now."

His mother's eyebrow rose over her left eye. "What did you do, Alex?"

"I made an ass out of myself, I'm afraid."

His mother snapped her fingers. "Give me her number. I will talk to her and make sure she knows what a great guy you are."

"No, Mom. This is something I need to fix."

She pulled him into a hug. "Tomorrow. Tonight, you need to be with family."

He spent the next two days coming back to the boy from many years ago. He helped his dad around the house, doing some repairs long neglected, enjoying the town he'd grown up in without the added pressure of Iron Rogue, and reconnecting with his parents and his life.

Revelations gave him a new perspective. Understanding came with his time there. Acceptance of his life and how it turned out made him realize things had never been as bad as he'd thought. His parents didn't hate him. His sisters didn't hate him. The biggest thing, he didn't hate himself.

What came as such a shock on that trip was he didn't hate himself for the path he'd chosen. He loved his music and his life, but he'd always wondered, in the back of his mind, if he'd made the wrong choice. The popularity of the band, the money, and the women—all of it said no. His happiness he'd questioned on several occasions. He realized now happiness wasn't always easy to achieve. The one thing missing might just be a brunette computer whiz in New York.

After he'd been there for three days, he decided it was time to go back and face Madison. He needed to make things right with her, for his own sake and hers. If she couldn't forgive him for being an ass, then he'd live with that and move on. He hoped she could see past all of his flaws to the real Alex. He wasn't perfect, never would be. The big thing was he cared for her, more than he realized. Madison in his life would make him happy, really happy.

But how to make her listen.

The entire plane ride back, he jotted down several ideas on how to win her back. Nothing seemed good enough or didn't fit with what he knew about Maddie. He could wine and dine her. That had turned out pretty well the first time. Too overdone now. He could whisk her away somewhere on the plane, somewhere romantic like Fiji, Hawaii, or Europe. He could lock them in his apartment until she told him she loved him.

His thoughts came to a screeching halt. Loved him? Did he love her? Was he willing to put all other women aside to spend the rest of his life with one?

He paced the small length of the plane as they zipped through the sky, the setting sun an orange, yellow, and red backdrop to his turmoil.

His butt hit the plane seat as he stared out the window for a second, thinking. Madison's face appeared before him in the reflection. Her smile lit up his heart when he thought about being with her, holding her, making love to her, and yes, spending the rest of his life waking up next to her.

"I love her."

The reflection of his face in the plane window revealed a wide grin. He *loved* her!

Without realizing his soul had been so upside down, he literally felt a calm washing over him. What Tori said had been right. Love meant everything.

Now, how to convince the one woman he hadn't been able to forget that he really did love her?

* * * *

Madison rubbed her tired eyes. She'd been in front of her computer for twenty-four hours solid, unable to think or function except on autopilot. *God, I hate that man!*

From what she knew, he'd disappeared to Iowa for a few days and no one had heard from him the entire time he was gone, not Noah, not Tori, no one. She didn't know whether to smack him upside his head or pull him into a hug and never let him go. *The jerk!*

The lights of the city had come on a few hours before as the night sky darkened into an inky black. Storms were predicted for tonight. The pounding rain would fit her mood perfectly along with her pint of Ben and Jerry's. Then sleep. Maybe she'd be able to hit deep sleep without dreaming. Exhaustion did that kind of thing sometimes.

She wearily climbed from her chair, flipped off the lights in her office, and headed for the kitchen for the ice cream. As she passed the windows that faced Alex's apartment, she noticed a light on in his living room. She stopped dead in her tracks, her heart pounding in her chest at the thought of him being close again. *He's home?*

The clock on the wall said nine. It was early for most people but not her tonight. She needed sleep in order to function around that devastatingly gorgeous guy. If she lost her mind with him, he'd pounce, make her body sing, tear out her heart, and be on his way. It was the way Alex Rockly worked. Right now, she couldn't handle him at his finest.

Lights flickered off, and the apartment was dark. A deep sigh escaped her mouth, calming her heart down a bit until she could function again. *Deep breaths. Deep breaths. I can do this.*

Ice cream in hand, she settled onto her couch and turned on the television to some chick flick movie she'd seen five thousand times. The mind numbing would be good.

A knock at the door woke her from where she'd fallen asleep against the back of the couch, the bowl of ice cream melted into a brown pool of chocolate and drool on her chin.

Another knock sounded, making her realize she sat in a fog for several moments. "Coming."

Who the hell could that be at this time of night? The peephole revealed her visitor.

Alex.

"What do you want?"

His voice low and growly sent shivers down her arms. "Can we talk?"

"Not a good idea, Alex."

"I really need to see you, Maddie, and I promise, it's not just for sex. I want to apologize."

"Apology accepted. Now go away."

"Please?"

God, I hate this! I hate him, but I love him too, and this is so not a good idea. She flicked open the lock on the door, slowly pulling it open to reveal him on the other side.

He looked like shit. Probably worse than she did.

"Can I come in?"

Her heart hammered in her chest. Bad idea for her to be alone with him, she knew that, but she couldn't tell him no. Her mouth wouldn't form the word as she stepped back, allowing him inside before she shut it behind her.

With her arms wrapped around her middle, she moved into the living room, taking a seat in the armchair so he couldn't sit beside her. "What do you want?"

He sat down on the couch across from her, his hands nervously moving over the thighs of his jeans. Even tired, he looked gorgeous. His gaze moved over her face, taking in everything as if he hadn't seen her for a long time. "I miss you."

She closed her eyes and sighed. "Please don't."

"I'm sorry. I need to start over, I guess." He dangled his hands between his knees and looked up. "I suppose Tori told you I went to Iowa for a few days."

"Yes."

"I did that because I needed to put something to rest with my parents that has been eating me alive for several years."

"I'm glad you were able to settle things then." She rose to her feet, hoping he would follow and leave her alone.

He didn't move.

She sat back down, tucking her legs beneath her and waited.

"Part of the reason I haven't been able to see myself with anyone on a long-term basis is because of what I do. A musician doesn't have much of a home life. We tour nonstop, we have women throwing themselves at us, the promoting, the interviews, all of that makes it difficult to show the person we love the kind of attention they deserve." He raked his fingers through his hair, frustration clear on his face. "I have been afraid of disappointing anyone I've even thought about having a relationship with. I couldn't stand to see that look on my parents' faces, and it kept me from committing to anyone."

"I don't understand."

"My father got me accepted to a prestigious architecture school right out of high school. He's an architect and wanted me to follow in his footsteps. I wanted to play guitar."

"I'm not following you."

Alex climbed to his feet, moving toward the sliding glass doors with his back to her. "The day we finished writing Dare to Love and recording it so it was perfect, I came home to share that with my parents. My dad handed me the acceptance letter. I blew up thinking they would never understand that I wanted to play music, not be an architect. I couldn't fathom the thought of not playing guitar. It is like the blood in my veins. I can't do anything else." He turned back to face her, his eyes distant and searching. "I walked away from my family that day. I didn't even talk to them for several years because of what I felt was their meddling in my life."

"But you are now, right?"

A small smile appeared on his lips. "Yeah, but I realize now how much I hurt them when I left. I didn't even know it, but my parents have been to some of our shows." He took his seat again. "I'm no psychologist, of course, but I think that's part of the reason I find it hard to be with one woman."

Sweeping a stray strand of hair behind her ear, she said, "I understand, Alex, I really do, but I want that in my life. I want someone who will be with me and only me. I'm old fashioned like that, I guess." Her gaze met his, taking in the look in his eyes she couldn't understand. "And I deserve to have that kind of love, the kind that lasts a lifetime."

His gaze fixed over her shoulder for a moment, making her uneasy as to where this conversation seemed to be headed. Did he want her? Yes, she knew that. Did he love her? She didn't think so. Alex wasn't the type of man who fell in love with anyone.

He pressed his lips together and rose to his feet. "I came here tonight to apologize and I've done that. I thought I knew where I was going with all of this, but I'm not sure anymore if I can give you what you want and what you deserve, Maddie." He brought her to her feet. "You mean a lot to me." He brushed his lips against hers, a small kiss, one that said more than she could have at that moment because her throat closed up with the threat of tears she was trying desperately not to shed in front of him. "Be happy, okay? That's all I want for you."

His footsteps faded as tears blurred her vision.

The echo of the door shutting softly behind him felt like a stake to the heart.

Alex was gone.

Chapter Fourteen

The first show of their new tour. Six weeks since she'd seen him.

Tori kept her up to date on the things going on with the band, how Dylan had made out with his injuries, and the legal stuff with stealing the car.

All the guys looked great up there. Iron Rogue was on it and more popular than ever.

What the hell am I doing here? He obviously doesn't want to see me or talk to me, or he would have called.

She stood in the shadows of the stage to the left, her eyes trained on the one man she couldn't forget.

Alex stood to the left of the microphone, his fingers flying over the strings like a man possessed. His focus was fixed on his guitar, paying no attention to anyone nearby, not the women, not the men—not anyone.

He'd left New York several weeks ago, locking up his apartment tight, never even saying goodbye before he'd gone. Not that she expected anything from him since she'd basically let him walk out of her life.

She'd been miserable ever since, not able to sleep properly, not able to eat worth shit, and work was almost nonexistent. Her boss even mentioned how badly her work progress had been over the last several weeks.

Her solution was to see him one last time. With Tori's help, she managed to get to the show and secure backstage passes. She wasn't sure if she could face him now that she stood near.

He looked good, all muscles, long hair, chiseled features, and the rock star persona down to a T. She wanted to touch him, run her hands over his jaw as she looked deep into his eyes, kiss his lips, and let him take her to ecstasy. She needed him.

A small hand on her arm brought her focus around to the woman standing beside her. Tori hugged her for several long minutes before releasing her so she could see her face.

"You look good, sad, but good."

"Thanks." Maddie looked down at Tori's outfit. The tight, short leather skirt and white flowing blouse looked fantastic on her. Wild curls framed her face, making her eyes look huge, and her lips look fuller. "You look gorgeous. Totally the rock star girlfriend."

Tori smiled and hugged her again. "You know I love you. You're good for my ego." The song changed onstage to a new song, something she'd never heard before. "You should listen to this."

"Why?"

"It's Alex's newest song. He wrote it several months ago." Tori bumped shoulders with her. "About the time you started seeing each other."

The melody seeped into her soul, taking her beyond the here and now to when they'd first met. The touch of his hand when he'd handed Tag back to her, the look in his eyes as they'd eaten their dinner together on his balcony, and finally the sadness he'd shown her when he'd left that last time. It was all there. The chords were raw, driving home the lyrics until your heart bled with the tears. She'd never heard something so tormented and soul-baring.

"He wrote this?"

"Yep, lyrics and all. This is totally him."

The title? Midnight Love.

"God, Tori. This is—" She couldn't even put the feelings into words. Madison looked up from where she stood, right into Alex's eyes. Her heart stopped for a beat before racing into a tempo she couldn't catch her breath on. He knew she stood there even if it was difficult to see her. The connection she felt with this man went beyond those of the heart. Their souls had found the one they were meant to be with for a lifetime.

She just needed to convince him of that.

The show wound down to the encore. Iron Rogue had killed their first show of the new tour. They'd be doing several in the US before moving onto a few overseas, including Germany, Switzerland, Denmark, Rome, and the UK.

The crowd went wild, chanting for more as the lights went down. Maddie could see the guys and Taylor move off the stage, heading for the stairs to the back where their dressing room stood waiting.

Madison had cut before them, making her way through the tunnel to the end near their dressing room, wanting to see the interaction of the guys with their fans. More so how Alex interacted with the women who undoubtedly would be throwing themselves at him.

At least a hundred people lined the walkway shouting their names and waving pictures, t-shirts, and flashing boobs as the guys broke through the doorway one by one. Noah led the group, stopping to talk to several people as he signed pictures, took photographs with the fans, and laughed with them, all the time keeping Tori close to his side. Aiden came next, flirting with each and every woman who stopped him with a hand on his arm, kissing their cheeks, taking more pictures, and hamming it up the only way Aiden knew how. Dylan followed, playing up his accident like a publicity stunt. It gave him something to talk about, show off his scars, and play the victim all the while keeping a close, secretive eye on Taylor who wasn't far behind him. Being the only woman in the band, Taylor had the popularity thing all tied up. The men backstage were there to see her, get her autograph, and pictures. She'd dressed the part of a female rock star and killed it with her tight jeans, bustier, and spiked hair. She was gorgeous.

Madison held her breath as she watched Alex clear the doorway trailing the rest of the group. His smile looked forced to her, something she wasn't used to seeing with him. He stopped and talked with everyone, signed posters, taking pictures, and making the rounds.

One thing she did notice. He avoided the women who were flashing naked breasts, who tried pulling him into a kiss, or those that paid a little too much attention to him. Odd behavior for the Alex Rockly she knew.

"Hey, Maddie," Noah said, ducking into the dressing room with Tori in tow like it was nothing to see her there.

Aiden and Dylan said hello as well, never missing a beat.

The second she met Alex's gaze, her world narrowed to only him. The rest of those standing nearby faded into nothingness.

"Hey."

"Hi. What are you doing here?" Alex asked, taking her hand, completely ignoring the people around them. Cameras flashed, people shouted his name, and nothing seemed to matter as his gaze took her in from her head to her boots.

She felt a smile tugging at her lips. "Tori got me tickets. I wanted to be at the first show."

A quick glance behind him, and then he pulled her inside their dressing room, shutting the door on the noise outside. Quiet surrounded them as she realized the others had left them alone, going on into the second room of their space where the venue had laid out more food than the whole group in the hall could eat. The low murmur of voices was barely heard over the buzzing in her ears.

"You look great."

"Thanks," she replied, wanting nothing more than to lose herself in him. "You too. You all sounded awesome."

"It was good, I think. The crowd seemed into it." He brought her further into the room, helping her to sit on the couch. "Can I get you something to drink or eat? There is all kinds of stuff in here. Name it." He turned to go get her something until she brought him to a halt with a grip on his hand.

"I'm good, Alex, but thanks. I ate before I came."

A nervous high surrounded him as he sat in the chair close to her, his knee brushing against her bare one where her skirt had ridden up to the middle of her thigh. "I'm glad you're here."

"You are?"

"Yeah." He reached for her hand, threading their fingers together in a tough grip, his gaze searching her face for what, she wasn't sure. "Listen, Maddie. I'm sorry about how things were left when we talked the last time."

"You needed time. I get that."

He ran his fingers down her cheek, stopping to brush them against the corner of her lip. His voice dropped to a rough whisper. "I should never have walked away from you. I was an idiot. I have been since the moment we met." A smile turned up his lips at the corners. "You mean more to me than any woman I have ever been with. You are so different from anyone I've been around, I wasn't sure what to do with you."

Her voice dropped to a murmur to match the quietness of his, dreading where he was headed with this line of talk. "Is this a bad thing?"

He chuckled as he threaded his hand behind her head, bringing her mouth within a hairsbreadth of his. The warmth of his breath on her mouth made her sigh with longing. A small touch was all she wanted, something to hold her over for the next hundred years if this didn't work out. Coming here, facing him might not have been the best decision she'd ever made.

He pressed his forehead against hers, his gaze fixed on hers. Emotion shone brightly for her to see.

His next words stopped her rapidly beating heart. "Madison Avery, I love you. You and I can be fantastic together if you let us. I'm not sure how this will work, but I want to try—with you—only you. I will do everything in my power to be the man you look for in your dreams. I can't pretend this won't be hard, you know that, but you can trust me to be faithful to you even in the face of the women we deal with on the road. I don't want anyone except you in my life and in my bed. The biggest thing holding me back from you was my fear of disappointing you. I don't ever want to hurt you."

Had he just said he loved her? *Oh shit.* A knot formed in her throat, making it difficult to answer his heartfelt declaration. A nod of her head was all she could manage for a minute.

He laughed. "Does that mean yes you'll be mine?"

She swallowed hard, forcing the lump away. "All I ever wanted was you, Alex. I love you."

The meeting of their mouths was something dreams were made of—hers. She'd always wanted to have this connection with one man, the only man for her, and now she did. Never in her wildest dreams did she imagine a man like Alex falling for her, but here they were declaring their love for each other, hoping their lives would sync together and they could live happily ever after.

Her breath became his as she opened her lips to the probing of the tip of his tongue. His low moan echoed hers, desire, need, and love beat through her veins hard enough to make her dizzy. He tilted her head with a hand on each cheek, driving his tongue further into her mouth, taking what he wanted, what they both wanted.

When their mouths parted, his gaze searched hers as he whispered, "Come back to the hotel with me. Please? Even if I can't make love to you, I want to hold you."

All she could do was nod. She needed his touch more than her next breath, and if he didn't make love to her soon, she might have to take matters into her own hands and seduce the hell out of him. A giggle of thought rushed through her brain. Seduce

Alex Rockly. That might be an interesting idea and one she could totally go with. "I will follow you anywhere."

"Guys? We're going back to the hotel. Catch up to you in the morning. Don't knock on the door or call."

Noah stuck his head in the room. "Great to see you, Maddie. Have fun." Tori giggled and smiled behind him as she waved.

Alex pulled her to her feet before wrapping a possessive arm around her waist. "We must run the gauntlet, my lady. The car waits outside. I'll send it back for the others after they drop us off." Alex pulled her in tighter. "Ready?"

"Is this the way it always is with you guys?"

"More times than not, yes." A frown pulled the corners of his mouth down. "Are you sure you're up to this? It can be a bit overwhelming."

"For you, I'd do anything." She grabbed her overnight bag from the floor, just in case.

"That's my girl!" He pulled open the door only to be met with absolute chaos. The crowd was stacked in there so tight, they could barely breathe, cameras and cell phones flashed, people shouted his name demanding the story, hands reached out for him, snagging his forearm, but every time he just shook them off, didn't say anything, and kept his gaze fixed on her face.

When they reached the side of the limo, the driver opened the door, but he stopped right before climbing in. "I love you." Framing her face with both of his hands, he leaned in and locked their mouths together in a panty-melting kiss.

Her hands gripped his forearms as he took the kiss deeper, sweeping away any doubts she had to the validity of his love as he staked his claim in front of everyone.

For now, she had accepted him with his chaotic life, and they would make it work. They had to.

Several minutes later the door to the suite he'd reserved at the hotel swept open to reveal a huge room. White leather couches, dark floors, white gauzy curtains on all the windows—

the place looked like a palace, a sterile one. Madison didn't care. It was a place for them to be alone.

They crossed the threshold hand in hand, seconds before he swept her up in his arms, and carried her toward what she assumed was the bedroom, her bag dangling from her fingers.

Gently laying her down on the bed, he moved over her positioning himself on her right side and rolling her toward him. His fingers trailed over her cheeks, her ear, down her neck, and across her shoulder before sliding slowly down her arm to take her hand in his. "I've missed you."

"I've missed you too."

"I'm sorry I was such an ass."

She closed her eyes for a second and smiled. "No more so than I was, Alex. We were trying to deny our feelings and protect our hearts. It's a natural human instinct."

"I hurt you. I never meant to do that.

"Yes, you did."

He opened his mouth, but she put a finger to his lips to stop his words.

"You meant to hurt me to push me away. You weren't ready to accept us, I know that. I wasn't happy about it, but I understood your reasons behind it." This was going to be tough. It had to be done though. "Rest assured you won't do it again. I won't allow you to hurt me over and over. I have more pride in myself to ever be your toy." She put one hand right over his heart. The organ hammered hard inside his chest. "I will cherish this forever. The love I feel for you will never die. That's not to say you can't hurt me beyond what my love for you can handle. Trust works both ways. I am trusting you with my love."

His eyes looked sad, almost hurt, but she had to say it, lay everything on the table because if she didn't, she would kick herself later for not protecting her heart.

When his gaze came back to her, she knew she didn't have to worry. He would never hurt her if it was at all possible for him to avoid.

"Maddie, I love you with all my heart. I never thought I would be able to say that to any woman." His fingers touched her cheek. "You are the perfect woman for me. You love me. That thought blows my mind. I can truly say I have no desire to be with anyone else or even look at anyone else. That thought scares me a little, but it's you, so I'm totally okay with it." He pressed a light kiss to the corner of her lips. "The logistics of this might be a bit difficult with your work and mine. We'll make it work somehow."

"What about my cats?"

"If I have to buy a separate bus just for the cats and us, I will. I'm not worried about it."

"Bus? You want me to travel with you?"

"As much as you can. I know your work requires some special times, Internet connections, or whatever. I'll put a damned satellite on top of the bus if I have to."

"Alex, I have more money than I could ever need in a lifetime. If I sell my apartment in New York for even half of what it is worth, I wouldn't have to worry about money."

"I have more than we could ever spend too, babe. What's mine is yours."

Unable to help herself, she had to tease him just a little. "You might want to think a little harder on that, Alex Rockly. If Rock Band News has the figures right, you're worth several million dollars. You never know, I could totally be a gold-digger."

He leaned in and kissed her hard. "If my sources are correct, Ms. Avery, you are too, so we are even."

"You checked me out?"

"Of course." He tangled his hand in her hair and brought their mouths closer. "I needed the perfect woman for me. One who is independent, takes no shit from me, can take care of herself without me, but lets me take care of her, and I don't ever have to worry about her financially if my career goes in the shitter tomorrow." He kissed her again. "Now, when we get married…"

Her breathing stopped. *Get married?*

"Yes, I said it. *When* we get married because it will happen eventually. No rush. Things are crazy right now, so I'm not going to ask officially, but it is in my plans." The brush of his mouth sent shivers to her toes. "We will worry about the financial side of things then. Right now, it's not even on my radar."

His knee crept between hers, taking possession of her lower body, as his hand landed on her hip.

"At this moment, I need to make love to you more than anything in this world. If you aren't okay with that, let me know. I can wait as long as I need to."

She grabbed the collar of his shirt, nipping at his mouth with her teeth as she whispered, "Make love to me, Alex. My dildo doesn't cut it when it comes to you."

"You are into toys? Why didn't you say so? I would love to drive you wild while I play with your body."

His mouth took possession one hundred percent, slanting over hers to get as close as he could. His hand cupped her breast through her blouse, thumbing her nipple through the thin shirt. Good Lord, the man knew how to touch her to bring her right up to moaning his name without a care.

The minute he released her mouth to skim along her cheek on his way to her ear, she gave into the sigh she held. "Alex."

Teeth and tongue did a number on her earlobe, driving her wild with need. The slight pain of his bite, soothed by the slip of his tongue until he moved onto her neck as she tilted her head to give him better access.

His hand left her breast, skimming along her side, over her hip, and up the inside of her thigh.

He lifted his head and smiled. "You aren't wearing underwear."

"I had high hopes for tonight."

"Naughty girl."

"Only for you."

His fingers slipped between her pussy lips to glance off her clit. Her body shook from head to toe at the sensation of his callused fingertip on her sensitive nub. A moan escaped her lips as she closed her eyes, relishing the touch of the man she loved.

"Open your eyes, babe. I want you to know who's touching you and bringing you to the brink of madness with his touch."

She slowly opened her eyes, only to drown in the blue of his. "I love you so much."

"And I love you. More than anything in this world. All I have belongs to you, heart, body, and soul." His murmured between kisses.

Two fingers pushed inside her, tearing a groan from her lips as she parted her thighs more. "I need you."

"You'll have me. Soon. First, you need to have a couple dozen orgasms."

He kissed his way down her body, stopping to open the buttons on her blouse before pushing her bra up in order to encompass the left nipple with his lips. She pushed her fingers into his hair, threading them along his scalp to hold him in place. Pain replaced by pleasure was the mantra of the day. He was going to drive her out of her mind before he finally gave her what she wanted. The slow suck on her nipple zinged straight to her clit. *Holy mother of God.*

"That's it, babe." He pushed two fingers inside her. "Let me feel your passion for me."

He pulled her nipple into his mouth, rubbing it against the top. A climax rolled over her, exploding as shards of colored glass behind her eyelids. "Alex!"

The minute she came down from her high, he pulled away to quickly shed his clothes, standing beside the bed in all his naked glory. Gorgeous wasn't word enough for Alex. His long hair hung down his back, but a few strands hanging over his chest almost touched his waist. His cock stood long and thick against his stomach, a small drop of pre-come glistened on the tip. She wanted his cock in her mouth. Sitting up, she scooted forward, framing his hips with her hands as she pulled him closer. With her palm wrapped around his girth, she slowly lowered her head toward the tip. He could stop her if he wanted, although she didn't know a man on earth that would say no to a blowjob.

"Do you want me to wear a condom, Angel?"

"Do I have anything to worry about?"

"No. I've always worn one before with everyone I've ever slept with, both during sex and oral."

She loved that he thought of her above anything else, even his own comfort. "Then I'm good." She licked up his entire length. "I want you to be able to feel everything I do."

The moment she took the tip between her lips, he tipped his head back as a deep, satisfying moan escaped his lips. Going down as far as she could without gagging, she met her lips on the way up with her hand, totally encompassing his length. The salty taste on her tongue wasn't unpleasant, but this was about Alex, not her. She wanted him to know this was something for him. The sting of his fists in her hair made her hotter than a firecracker on the fourth of July. The smell of him, the taste of him, the feel of him stretching her mouth as she gave him pleasure, drove everything home. This was Alex. He was hers.

After several moments, he forced her to stop with a pull on her hair. "I'll come in your mouth if you keep that up. It feels too good and I want to be inside you when I come." He leaned over her, forcing her to lie back on the bed. "Roll over so I can take this sexy little skirt off you."

She showed him her back, loving the slow draw on the zipper while he took it down, and then the shimmying of the skirt when he pulled it off her hips, and down her legs, baring her naked ass to his hot gaze.

His warm palm skimmed over her skin. "You have a gorgeous ass, babe. Someday we are gonna take this for a ride. It's too hot, not to." He smacked her left butt cheek, not hard, but enough to sting slightly. "Ever had a man in your ass?"

"Once. It wasn't a pleasant experience."

"I'll make sure you enjoy it when it's us. If it's not done right, it's not pleasurable for the woman."

His tongue slid up her spine, pushing her blouse out of the way, and leaving goosebumps in its wake. A twist of his fingers and her bra lay limp under her. Butterfly kisses swished across her shoulder blades. Nips along the top of her shoulders had her sighing in pleasure. The man knew how to make love.

"On your back, please. I want to taste you all the way to your gorgeous feet."

"You have a foot fetish?" She giggled at the thought. Never in a million years could she imagine Alex with any kind of fetish, much less feet.

"I have a *you* fetish, all of you."

No one had ever said anything so sweet before. No wonder she loved this man.

He proceeded to kiss every inch of her from the tip of her nose to the soles of her feet, licking, nipping, and soothing away the sting as he went. The one place she wanted him the most was ignored, creating a deep need inside her she couldn't control. "Alex, please."

He glanced up from his place at the foot of the bed, a silly little grin on his mouth. "Did I miss something?"

Her back bowed as she spread her legs. "I want your mouth on me."

"Where?"

"My pussy. I want your mouth on my pussy."

"Hmm."

The second his warm tongue touched her center, the moan she'd kept trapped in her chest burst loose in a long, low sound of need.

"Now, there is a nice sound." He hummed his pleasure against the inside of her right thigh. "I do like that."

"Please. I need you to make me come. I'm going to burst into flames if you don't hurry."

"Oh no. Hurrying isn't on my agenda."

He proceeded to lick and suck at her center until she was squirming beneath him, desperate to climax. Every time she got close, he'd back off, only licking lightly to keep her on the edge without letting her go over. "I'm going to hurt you, Alex, badly if you don't make me come."

"Threats, huh?" He glanced to the open bag that she'd brought with them from the venue. She'd forgotten about the toys she'd packed. "Oh, this looks like fun." He turned on a small bullet vibrator, she really hadn't had a chance to use much. When she had, it had made her come so hard, she saw stars. The low hum of the toy made her shiver in anticipation.

He took the vibrator and slowly pushed it into her cunt.

Fuuuck!

The groan escaping her lips sounded animalistic and raw. Thankfully, she wouldn't last long if he kept things at this pace, she was so close. The second he wrapped his lips around her clit and bit down, she exploded in shards of light, busting into a rain of color behind her eyelids. His name came out in a low growl.

"That was nice. Shall we go again?" he asked, pulling the bullet from inside her.

"Fuck no, mister." She grabbed at his shoulders, yanking until he moved up her body. "Come up here. I need you inside me."

"Music to my ears, Angel." He kissed his way up her abdomen, positioning himself between her thighs as the crown of his cock nudged at her entrance. "Welcome me home, sweetheart."

"Welcome home, Alex."

Epilogue

Last night of their tour. The crowd chanted in epic rhythm to their signature song. His world was complete. He had his woman, his world, by his side, and couldn't be happier than he was tonight.

The plans he'd made were in place. It would be the best night of his life.

Notes faded on a sigh. The crowd seemed to know something was up as the sound stop. Quiet descended.

Alex stepped up to the microphone. Everyone knew about tonight except her. The ultimate secret had been kept. "Thank you for tonight, folks. This tour has been larger-than-life, and we couldn't have done it without you."

The crowd went wild, chanting Iron Rogue for several moments until Alex raised his hand.

"I do ask your patience for just a second." He turned toward his side of the stage and motioned for Maddie to come out from her hiding spot behind the curtain.

"Me?" she mouthed, and he nodded.

She slowly walked out dressed to the nines in her tight red dress hugging every curve he knew so well. The stilettos on her feet brought her closer to his height and made her legs look killer.

Noise exploded throughout the arena. Not that they didn't know he and Maddie were a couple, they'd been together going on six months, but other than pictures, she was rarely seen, preferring to stay in the shadows.

Not tonight.

"Everyone, this is Maddie."

She blushed as she buried her face in his shoulder. "What are you doing?" she whispered. "You know I hate this."

"I know, babe, but this is special." He pulled his guitar off his shoulder, handing it to the roadie who appeared at his side. "Thanks, man."

"Alex?"

He dropped to one knee in front of her, pulling out a red velvet ring box from inside his jeans pocket. Her eyes widened as her face paled when he opened the box. "Madison Avery. I feel like I've loved you for a lifetime already but not long enough. I want to spend the rest of my life taking care of you, loving you, making babies with you, and showing the world love exists even for rock stars. Will you marry me?"

Her hands flew up, covering her mouth as several tears slipped down her cheeks. Her head nodded up and down, even though she didn't speak the words.

"You have to say it, babe. I won't take anything less."

She leaned in and brought the microphone closer. "Yes!" Her shouted answer echoed throw the rafters as he climbed to his feet and slipped the ring on her finger. "He's off the market, ladies. Sorry."

The crowd clapped and shouted, bringing a smile to his lips. Leave it to his Maddie to upstage the main act.

She jumped into his arms, letting him wrap her in a squeezing hug meant to solidify their joining. Letting her go hadn't been an option for several months, and now he never had to. She was his forever, and forever wouldn't be long enough.

The dream was real, and he'd found his happily ever after.

The End

About the Author

Sandy Sullivan is a romance author, who, when not writing, spends her time with her husband Shaun on their farm in middle Tennessee. She loves to ride her horses, play with their dogs and relax on the porch, enjoying the rolling hills of her home south of Nashville. Country music is a passion of hers and she loves to listen to it while she writes, although when she writes sex scenes, it has to be completely quiet.

She is an avid reader of romance novels and enjoys reading Nora Roberts, Jude Deveraux and Susan Wiggs. Finding new authors and delving into something different helps feed the need for literature. A registered nurse by education, she loves to help people and spread the enjoyment of romance to those around her with her novels. She loves cowboys so you'll find many of her novels have sexy men in tight jeans and cowboy boots. This newest passion includes rock stars who are moody, but need to find the woman of their dreams too.

www.romancestorytime.com